Praise for Johnny Townsend

In *Zombies for Jesus*, "Townsend isn't writing satire, but deeply emotional and revealing portraits of people who are, with a few exceptions, quite lovable."

Kel Munger, *Sacramento News and Review*

Townsend's stories are "a gay *Portnoy's Complaint* of Mormonism. Salacious, sweet, sad, insightful, insulting, religiously ethnic, quirky-faithful, and funny."

D. Michael Quinn, author of *The Mormon Hierarchy: Origins of Power*

Johnny Townsend is "an important voice in the Mormon community."

Stephen Carter, editor of *Sunstone* magazine

T0059394

"Told from a believably conversational first-person perspective, [*The Abominable Gayman*'s] novelistic focus on Anderson's journey to thoughtful self-acceptance allows for greater character development than often seen in short stories, which makes this well-paced work rich and satisfying, and one of Townsend's strongest. An extremely important contribution to the field of Mormon fiction." Named to Kirkus Reviews' Best of 2011.

Kirkus Reviews

"The thirteen stories in *Mormon Underwear* capture this struggle [between Mormonism and homosexuality] with humor, sadness, insight, and sometimes shocking details....*Mormon Underwear* provides compelling stories, literally from the inside-out."

Niki D'Andrea, *Phoenix New Times*

The Circumcision of God "asks questions that are not often asked out loud in Mormonism, and certainly not answered."

Jeff Laver, author of *Elder Petersen's Mission Memories*

"Johnny Townsend's short stories cannot be pigeon-holed. His keen observations on the human condition come in many shapes and sizes...reflecting on both his Jewish and Mormon backgrounds as well as life in the vast and varied American gay community. He dares to think and write about people and incidents that frighten away more timid artists. His perspective is sometimes startling, sometimes hilarious, sometimes poignant, but always compassionate."

Gerald S. Argetsinger, Artistic Director of the Hill Cumorah Pageant (1990-96)

The Circumcision of God is "a collection of short stories that consider the imperfect, silenced majority of Mormons, who may in fact be [the Church's] best hope....[The book leaves] readers regretting the church's willingness to marginalize those who best exemplify its ideals: those who love fiercely despite all obstacles, who brave challenges at great personal risk and who always choose the hard, higher road."

Kirkus Reviews

In *Mormon Fairy Tales*, Johnny Townsend displays "both a wicked sense of irony and a deep well of compassion."

Kel Munger, *Sacramento News and Review*

"*Selling the City of Enoch* exists at that awkward intersection where the LDS ideal meets the real world, and Townsend navigates his terrain with humor, insight, and pathos."

Donna Banta, author of *False Prophet*

The Golem of Rabbi Loew will prompt "gasps of outrage from conservative readers...a strong collection."

Kirkus Reviews

"That's one of the reasons why I found Johnny Townsend's new book *Mormon Fairy Tales* SO MUCH FUN!! Without fretting about what the theology is supposed to be if it were pinned down, Townsend takes you on a voyage to explore the rich-but-undertapped imagination of Mormonism. I loved his portrait of spirit prison! He really nailed it—not in an official doctrine sort of way, but in a sort of 'if you know Mormonism, you know this is what it must be like' way—and what a prison it is!

Johnny Townsend has written at least ten books of Mormon stories. So far, I've read only two (*Mormon Fairy Tales* and *The Circumcision of God*), but I'm planning to read the rest—and you should too, if you'd like a fun and interesting new perspective on Mormons in life and imagination!"

C. L. Hanson, *Main Street Plaza*

In *Let the Faggots Burn*, "Townsend's heart-rending descriptions of the victims…seem to [make them] come alive once more."

Marginal Mormons is "an irreverent, honest look at life outside the mainstream Mormon Church….Throughout his musings on sin and forgiveness, Townsend beautifully demonstrates his characters' internal, perhaps irreconcilable struggles….Rather than anger and disdain, he offers an honest portrayal of people searching for meaning and community in their lives, regardless of their life choices or secrets." Named to Kirkus Reviews' Best of 2012.

"The Sneakover Prince" from *God's Gargoyles* is "one of the most sweet and romantic stor[ies] I have ever read."

"*Let the Faggots Burn* is a one-of-a-kind piece of history. Without Townsend's diligence and devotion, many details would've been lost forever. With his tremendous foresight and tenacious research, Townsend put a face on this tragedy at a time when few people would talk about it….Through Townsend's vivid writing, you will sense what it must've been like in those final moments as the fire ripped through the UpStairs Lounge. *Let the Faggots Burn* is a chilling and insightful glimpse into a largely forgotten and ignored chapter of LGBT history."

Robert Camina, writer and producer of the documentary *Raid of the Rainbow Lounge*

The stories in *The Mormon Victorian Society* "register the new openness and confidence of gay life in the age of same-sex marriage….What hasn't changed is Townsend's wry, conversational prose, his subtle evocations of character and social dynamics, and his deadpan humor. His warm empathy still glows in this intimate yet clear-eyed engagement with Mormon theology and folkways. Funny, shrewd and finely wrought dissections of the awkward contradictions—and surprising harmonies—between conscience and desire." Named to Kirkus Reviews' Best of 2013.

Kirkus Reviews

"Johnny Townsend's 'Partying with St. Roch' [in the anthology *Latter-Gay Saints*] tells a beautiful, haunting tale."

Kent Brintnall, Out in Print: Queer Book Reviews

"The struggles and solutions of the individuals [in *Latter-Gay Saints*] will resonate across faith traditions and help readers better understand the cost of excluding gay members from full religious participation."

Publishers Weekly

"This collection of short stories [*The Mormon Victorian Society*] featuring gay Mormon characters slammed in the face from the first page, wrestled my heart and mind to the floor, and left me panting and wanting more by the end. Johnny Townsend has created so many memorable characters in such few pages. I went weeks thinking about this book. It truly touched me."

Tom Webb, judge for The Rainbow Awards (A Bear on Books)

Dragons of the Book of Mormon is an "entertaining collection....Townsend's prose is sharp, clear, and easy to read, and his characters are well rendered..."

Publishers Weekly

"The pre-eminent documenter of alternative Mormon lifestyles…Townsend has a deep understanding of his characters, and his limpid prose, dry humor and well-grounded (occasionally magical) realism make their spiritual conundrums both compelling and entertaining. [*Dragons of the Book of Mormon* is] [a]nother of Townsend's critical but affectionate and absorbing tours of Mormon discontent." Named to Kirkus Reviews' Best of 2014.

Kirkus Reviews

"Mormon Movie Marathon," from *Selling the City of Enoch*, "is funny, constructively critical, but also sad because the desire…for belonging is so palpable."

Levi S. Peterson, author of *The Backslider* and *The Canyons of Grace*

Selling the City of Enoch is "sharply intelligent…pleasingly complex…The stories are full of…doubters, but there's no vindictiveness in these pages; the characters continuously poke holes in Mormonism's more extravagant absurdities, but they take very little pleasure in doing so….Many of Townsend's stories…have a provocative edge to them, but this [book] displays a great deal of insight as well…a playful, biting and surprisingly warm collection."

Kirkus Reviews

Gayrabian Nights is "an allegorical tour de force...a hard-core emotional punch."

Gay. Guy. Reading and Friends

In *Gayrabian Nights*, "Townsend's prose is always limpid and evocative, and...he finds real drama and emotional depth in the most ordinary of lives."

Kirkus Reviews

"Among the most captivating of the prose [in *Off the Rocks*, in a piece reprinted from the collection *A Day at the Temple*] was a story by Johnny Townsend illustrating two Mormon missionaries who break the rules of their teachings to spend more time with one another."

Lauren Childers, *Windy City Times*

Gayrabian Nights is a "complex revelation of how seriously soul damaging the denial of the true self can be."

Ryan Rhodes, author of *Free Electricity*

In *Lying for the Lord*, Townsend "gets under the skin of his characters to reveal their complexity and conflicts....shrewd, evocative [and] wryly humorous."

Kirkus Reviews

Missionaries Make the Best Companions

Johnny Townsend

BookLocker.com, Inc.
2015

First Edition

Cover design by Todd Engel

Dedicated to those who bring love and peace to the world, whatever the risk

Special thanks to Donna Banta

for her editorial assistance

Contents

Introduction:

Preserving Mormon Culture

When I first began reading the stories of Isaac Bashevis Singer, I was instantly fascinated. He had so thoroughly described a culture which in just a few years had become completely extinct. Yes, Jews survived, but Eastern European shtetl Jewry did not. There were serious problems in that culture, to be sure, recounted in detail, but there was a real beauty as well.

As an eleven-year-old boy in New Orleans in the summer of 1973, I watched a horrifying news story of thirty-two people who died trying to escape a French Quarter bar which had been set on fire by an arsonist. The images of people burning to death halfway out the windows haunted me for years. When I came out as gay in the late 1980's and learned for the first time that the UpStairs Lounge had been a gay bar, and that the arson had occurred on Gay Pride Day, the horror of that day came rushing back. I wanted to read more about it, but there was nothing to read.

So I decided to write something myself. I tracked down survivors of the fire and friends and relatives of those who had been killed, and I tried to tell the stories of the people who'd been in the bar that night before those stories were lost forever. This was at the height of the AIDS epidemic, before any successful treatment existed, and people in my community were dying daily. That book, *Let the Faggots Burn*, may not be my best writing, but I consider it a useful historical document.

Now, twenty-five years after I wrote my account, other people are telling the story in new books and in documentaries, and they are thankfully learning information I didn't know, but the vast majority of my interviews with people involved in the fire simply can't be replicated given that so many of them have since died.

I recorded history, however inadequately. That feels like something important.

I suppose in many ways, this is the same motivation behind my writing Mormon short story collections. With the advent of the internet, so much information about Church history is now available, and Mormons are leaving the Church by the thousands and tens of thousands as they learn that much of what they had always been taught simply isn't true. Other religions also have issues with their past, of course. Catholics have the Inquisition, to mention just one. Yet even something as horrific as that didn't destroy Catholicism.

But the situation for Mormons is slightly different. We have absolute proof that some of the scripture Joseph Smith claimed to translate from Egyptian papyri was completed fabricated. We know because we still have those papyri, which have been translated correctly now by Egyptologists. There is DNA evidence which proves the Native Americans did not come from the Middle East as the Book of Mormon claims. We have documents which prove Joseph Smith lied about his polygamy, even to members of his Church, and was married to girls as young as fourteen. At some point, even "faith" isn't enough to prevent members from realizing the whole thing might really be just a great big sham.

And yet, despite the many problems I have with Mormon doctrine and social practices, I also had many wonderful experiences as a member of that Church, and I truly don't want to see it dwindle away completely. Improve, yes, but disappear, no.

So I write about Mormons. True believers are horrified by my work and won't touch it, and many ex-Mormons are so "over" religion that they certainly don't want to read stories about it now. So I'm not sure I'll ever have much of an audience. But it feels important to me to record the culture honestly. I understand Mormons, both their strengths and their weaknesses, and I believe they are people worth knowing.

Jewish culture lived on despite the destruction of the shtetl. Gay culture survived the death of many of its greatest artists from AIDS. And Mormonism will probably continue on as well. But there is no doubt it will be changed by the current events shaping it just as those other cultures were.

I write stories to entertain, as any writer does. But I also write them to record.

That attempt gives me comfort, even if few other people in Mormon culture have any desire to read my books. As a writer, I obviously want my work to be known, but ultimately, I write out of the belief that history and experience are things worth preserving, and in the hope that if something is recorded well, it never really dies.

Under the Covers

Elder Zachary's dislike for me started the minute I walked into the Rome Four apartment in the northeastern part of the city. I'd just caught the ferry from Sardinia to Civitavecchia, tossed about the entire time by a winter storm, then boarded a train to the Stazione Termini in Rome, and finally caught a bus to my new apartment. By anyone's standards, I should have been exhausted and maybe even in a foul mood, especially since it had been cold and raining heavily all day. But I was smiling. And I could tell in an instant that Elder Zachary disliked me for it.

"You seem to be in an awfully good mood," he said. "Troppo allegro. What mission rules did you break while you were all alone?"

"What makes you think I was all alone?" I said with a grin. "The ferry was an overnight trip."

The other missionaries gasped at my joke, but Elder Zachary's eyes grew tighter. "You would have had a man share your bunkroom. Are you admitting you're a finocchio?"

I shrugged. "Desperate times for call desperate measures." I wasn't gay, of course, but my new senior zone leader was beginning to get on my nerves after only a few moments. "Now, if you don't mind, I'd like to get to know my new companion more intimately." I paused. "I mean, better." I made an elaborate wink, grabbed my two suitcases, and nodded for my new assignment, Elder Burton, to show me the way to our room. He looked like he'd just heard he'd been disfellowshipped, but he swallowed and led the way.

Once in the tiny room, I put my suitcases down next to my cot and closed the door. "Is he always such a prick?"

"D-don't speak ill of the Lord's anointed," was all he could say.

"Elder Burton, I'm not gay. I have a testimony. I've baptized eight people so far on my mission, twice the average. You can relax."

"O-okay, Elder Hardinger."

I unpacked in just five minutes, there not being much to it. Then I turned back to Elder Burton, who was standing beside his desk, still looking worried. "I've had a long day," I said, "but I still think we'll be better off away from the apartment than hanging around Elder Zachary while he waits for the new junior ZL to arrive. So what say you show me to our tracting zone?" I was the senior, after all, having been out twenty months already. This would probably be my last area before I went home to Pennsylvania.

He nodded, I offered a short prayer, and we headed for the front door. "Teach a lesson tonight," Elder Zachary called out as I reached for the door knob.

"There's no reason you can't be doing some cold calling," I said in return. "Follow the Spirit and use the phone book. No sense wasting the Lord's time."

Elder Burton looked at me in horror.

I shrugged again as I closed the door behind us.

We had to catch two buses to reach our area. I tried to memorize all the landmarks as quickly as possible so I'd be able to do this on my own if my companion were transferred next month. From the look on his face, I was sure he hoped he would be. I wasn't a bad guy, though, in my own humble opinion, and hoped I could win him over. After so many months as a Mormon missionary, I'd simply grown tired of the "unrighteous dominion" under which we suffered constantly. The mission president had ordered all the sister missionaries to cut their hair short so they wouldn't waste time trying to look pretty. They were here to work, after all, not attract men. The president had also ordered the elders to wear their suit jackets all year long, even during the sweltering summer months, because he was sure it made us look more righteous.

And it wasn't only the rules from the top that were unreasonable. The zone leaders and district leaders took their calling as mission leaders quite seriously as well. I'd been ordered to work an extra ten hours a week to show the Lord my dedication, when the normal sixty hours was plenty already. I'd been ordered to wake up at 5:30 instead of 6:00, to show my eagerness for the work day. I'd been ordered to stand up in church and confess all my weaknesses, to show the local members how humble I was. While I still believed the Church was true, as I'd just told my companion, I nevertheless had serious doubts about the methods our leaders sometimes used to lead.

As it turned out, Elder Burton and I did teach a lesson that night, about Joseph Smith's First Vision in the Sacred Grove. It was possible to go an entire week without teaching, so I was grateful for Heavenly Father's blessing in leading us to a receptive person. And since leaders weren't the only imperfect

7

Mormons, I had to admit I looked forward to telling Elder Zachary about it later.

"How did you do tonight?" were the first words out of his mouth when we entered the apartment. He and his new companion were standing at their bedroom door in their garments. Their bedroom, naturally, was the apartment's living room. The other companionship shared the regular-sized bedroom, and the tiny room Elder Burton and I shared looked like the nursery. Mission royalty always claimed the living room as their own space. I don't suppose I minded for the most part, except when the leaders were so obnoxious. It looked like the zone leaders hadn't been out the entire evening. But then, I was probably just making assumptions.

"Taught the first discussion," said Elder Burton with a hesitant smile.

Elder Zachary ignored him and continued looking at me. "Soltanto uno?" he said. "If you guys had faith, you could have taught three colloqui." His continual mixture of English and Italian was beginning to annoy me. Couldn't he just pick one language and stick with it?

"How many did you teach sitting around here in your underwear?" I returned. "Any luck on the phone?"

Elder Zachary's eyes narrowed again. "This isn't about luck," he said. "This is about faith. You could baptize a hundred people a month if you had enough fede."

I looked at Elder Burton, whose eyes were wide as he anticipated the interaction. I motioned for him to go on to our bedroom, and he did so willingly. Then I turned back to my zone leader. "First of all," I said slowly, "if that were true, you've just admitted that *you* obviously don't have any faith. But secondly, it's *not* true. I can't force someone to accept the gospel. I'm here to offer it to them. It's up to them whether they're interested or not."

"Everyone is interested," Elder Zachary replied. "They just need to feel the Spirit to realize it. And if you can't provide the Spirit, the fact that they don't get battezzati is on you."

I sighed. Elder Zachary wasn't the first leader to say this kind of thing. I'd believed it for a long time and spent months and months feeling guilty, until I realized it was a lie. I wasn't about to put up with that kind of thinking any longer. "I'm not responsible for decisions other people make."

"Are you calling the mission president a liar?" Elder Zachary put his hands on his hips. I saw the tiniest twitch in his garments near his crotch. He was getting off on being a jackass.

"I can't make people join," I said.

"You're *allowing* them to join," he returned. "They are ready now but just need a spiritual experience in order to realize it. It's up to you to provide that for them."

"I'm just here to offer," I insisted.

"I'm going to have to report you to the presidente," Elder Zachary said coldly. "Here we are about to get a temple in Rome, and you're bringing us all down."

"Are you saying the Lord made a mistake by calling me to this mission?" I asked.

Elder Zachary suddenly began to smile wickedly. "If you're right and I'm wrong," he said, "why did the Lord call *me* to be a zone leader, while you're about to finish your mission, and you're still just a measly senior companion?"

And then it happened. All my bravado slipped right out of me, and the habitual tonnage of everyday Mormon guilt came rushing back. Maybe *I* was the one being an ass, I thought. The Church *was* true, after all, and that meant Heavenly Father had, in fact, called Elder Zachary to the position he held over me. "All right, all right," I said. "I'll teach five lessons tomorrow, okay?"

"See that you do." I was almost sure I heard him mutter "stronzo" as I left the room. It was the same thing I was thinking about him.

Over the next few days, I tried to act simultaneously gung ho and contrite. Elder Zachary seemed to tolerate me slightly better, but his eyes still narrowed most of the time he deigned to look in my direction. On the chore rotation, it was his week to cook, and he'd asked all of us up front what we specifically liked and disliked. I thought this surprisingly admirable of him, since most missionaries simply cooked what they wanted and to hell with what anybody else thought. Maybe we'd just gotten off on the wrong foot. But on the third day, I finally realized his motives hadn't been quite as altruistic as I'd hoped. Both Elder Burton and I had admitted a dislike for liver, the other three elders hadn't specified either a like or dislike for it, but liver is what we had for lunch. Since we only had two meals a day— breakfast on our own when we woke up in the morning and a communal lunch at 2:00—a distasteful dinner could throw off the entire evening.

I wasn't going to let Elder Zachary feel too victorious, though, so I ate every bite with a smile, forced as it was. Elder Burton only ate a few bites of his and then excused himself.

"This is not so bad, after all," I said then, scooping the remains of my companion's meal onto my plate and finishing it off.

I could tell by that sadistic smile of Zachary's that he wasn't fooled, so I probably suffered for nothing.

That evening, Elder Burton and I took a break from tracting so I could treat him to some pizza at a shop that sold it by the slice.

The next day was worse. For lunch, Elder Zachary proudly presented us each with a peanut butter and jelly sandwich. The others exclaimed in grateful awe at the sight. Peanut butter was almost impossible to find in Italy, so this meal represented a great deal of effort on Zachary's part. "I just thought it would be a treat to have some genuine comfort food," he said with that special smile of his.

Since I'd told him at the beginning of the week that I was allergic to peanuts, it was clear what his real agenda was.

"I had your serving of liver yesterday," I said to Elder Burton. "It's only fair you have my sandwich today. I'll fast instead for the Spirit to guide us to a special family."

"It's against the rules to fast more than once a month," said Elder Zachary.

I wanted to say, "It's also against the rules to try to murder other missionaries," but I was still trying to understand the real reason the Lord had chosen this man to guide me. There was obviously something I was missing, and I needed to humble myself to figure it out. I just smiled serenely and went to my desk to review one of the discussions.

It was my day to wash dishes, and I had to laugh that despite the simple meal, Elder Zachary had still managed to get over half the dishes in the kitchen dirty. I asked my companion to offer a prayer in our room after I was done, and then we headed out the door.

Elder Burton was exceptionally quiet on the ride to our tracting zone, the bus windows so covered in frigid condensation we almost missed our stop. But while we were climbing up the stairs to the sixth floor of the first building on our list, he said simply, "Elder Hardinger, I'm thinking of going home."

"What?" I said, surprised.

"I'm not sure I believe any more."

This happened all the time with the local members. And with friends and even family back home. But it didn't happen often with missionaries. "Is it the polygamy?" I asked. "Or the lack of DNA evidence for the Lamanites?"

He shook his head. "I don't care about any of that. I understand the necessity of faith." We reached the top floor and stopped to take a breath.

"Then what is it?" I panted.

"I'm just not having any fun."

I looked at him. "Is this supposed to be fun?" I asked.

He shrugged. "Maybe fun isn't the right word. I just mean…we're spending every waking minute with the elect. The best of the best. People who have dedicated their time and money to serving the Lord. And…"

I nodded for him to continue.

"Half of them are assholes," he said firmly, "and most of the others are just average joes, nothing special. That's got to say something about the whole thing."

"Well," I said carefully, feeling the weight of my position as senior companion, "we're just kids, aren't we? Still teenagers. You can't expect us all to behave like bishops and stake presidents."

Elder Burton shook his head sadly. "When you first came to the district, I had such hope that finally, someone was going to stand up to Zachary. He's such a bully. I was here with him for two months before you came." He turned to look back down the stairs. "I had such hope."

I was surprised, never having suspected a thing. Now I felt guilty all over again. But while I'd often experienced many of Elder Burton's thoughts myself over the past year and a half, I'd still always figured the point was to learn from all this. One could learn from a sterling example, but one could also learn from a poor one. Earth life was a classroom, and every lesson was for our benefit. I'd heard that in Sunday School. And Seminary. And Priesthood. And the Missionary Training Center.

We tracted out the building, unsuccessfully, and once back on the street, I said, "I'm not in the mood. Too hungry. Are you up for more pizza?"

Elder Burton grinned. "How can you afford it?"

"I have my own personal debit card. I worked hard to save up money for my mission, and I'm not limiting myself to the pre-ordained missionary budget."

"Why can't you be a rebel like this all the time?" He was joking, but I thought about his words the entire time we were eating.

It was exceptionally cold this evening, with a stiff wind, so after the pizza I led Elder Burton to a bar where we drank some hot chocolate. I enjoyed the break, but I was beginning to feel guilty again. I felt bad for following the rules, and I felt bad for breaking them. What other option did that leave me? Were people like us destined to feel miserable no matter what? Were we just bad people, and that's what we got?

"I've seen you guys around."

I turned and saw a young man in his early twenties, standing with his cup of coffee. I put on my missionary smile.

"You guys seem nice."

It's all an act, I wanted to tell him.

"I'm kind of searching right now. Do you guys think you could teach me something?"

I looked at Elder Burton and he looked at me, and then we stood up and followed the young man two blocks to his building. We taught our first discussion to Dario, each of us bearing our testimony at the appropriate places, and then made a return appointment to see the young man again in two days. As we left the building, Elder Burton said, "Maybe it *is* true."

I didn't know what to say to that, so we walked to the bus stop in silence. We could see a bus just pulling away, so we knew we had several minutes to wait before the next one came along. We watched the traffic pass, still lost in our own thoughts. Finally, after about ten minutes, Elder Burton turned to me. "Do you know what he told me?"

"Who?" I asked.

"Elder Zachary."

"I can't imagine," I said.

Elder Burton sighed heavily. "He came in the bathroom one day while I was showering." He looked me straight in the eye. "He said…I had a little dick."

My mouth fell open.

"He said it was a punishment for not being valiant in the Pre-Existence. I was good enough to be born into a Mormon family in America, but not *quite* good enough to have all the blessings that people like him received."

"You should have slugged him."

He looked down at the ground. "I gave in, just like you did." He paused. "It's what good boys do, isn't it." It wasn't a question.

"It's only one guy," I said.

"Is it?" asked Elder Burton. "You hear stories about some of the apostles, too. They just try to keep everything under cover." He paused again. "Elder Zachary will probably become an apostle one day." He looked like his dog had just died.

A gust of icy wind buffeted us, and I wanted to hug my companion to keep him from feeling so cold.

We waited another twenty minutes for the next bus, arriving home just after 9:40. "Teach any lessons?" asked Elder Zachary as we came in the door.

"Yes," I said softly, heading with my companion to our room.

"Get a return appointment?" he persisted. "Qualcosa utile?"

"Yes."

Once we were in our room, I closed the door behind us, looking at the door knob longingly. It was against mission rules to lock our doors. Our leaders had to be able to come in at any moment to verify we weren't committing the serious sin of studying on our beds, or, God forbid, the unpardonable sin of masturbating. I knew we were supposed to study until lights out at 10:30, but I really wasn't in the mood tonight. I just wanted to plop into bed and forget about everything.

"Elder Hardinger!"

"What?"

"Look!" Elder Burton pointed to my bed. I turned and saw that my two blankets were missing. All that was left was a thin sheet. And our building only received about two hours of heat a day, one hour in the morning, starting at 7:00, and another hour at night, starting at 9:00. Even with the heat on at this moment, it wasn't terribly warm in the room.

I marched out of the bedroom toward the ZL's room. "Where are my blankets?" I demanded.

Elder Zachary had that sickening smile I knew so well. "We're having a baptism tomorrow morning," he explained. "So I spent the evening at the chapel filling the font, and we have to keep the water covered to keep it from getting cold."

"And you're using *my* blankets because…?"

"Because you need to learn to sacrifice for the gospel."

"And *you've* already learned that lesson."

He smiled.

I went to the kitchen, where the other elders were gathered around the table, eating stale bread and jam. I looked on my shelf for my Bucaneve cookies, but the package was missing. I returned to my room. Elder Burton was in his garments, kneeling beside his bed, crying softly. I sat on his bed and put my hand on his shoulder. He opened his eyes and looked at me, shaking his head forlornly.

"I'm going home," he said, choking a little on his words.

I leaned over until our heads were almost touching. "Give me a few more days," I replied. Elder Burton looked at me with the saddest eyes I'd ever seen. Then he pushed me aside and climbed into bed, nodding at me to turn out the light.

I sat at my desk in the dark, keeping my eyes on our glow-in-the-dark clock, until 11:30. Then I took off my suit, quietly opened the bedroom door, and tiptoed down the hall. I crept into the ZL's bedroom and stood over Elder Zachary's bed. I might get sent home for this, but I knew I had to do it.

I gently lifted Elder Zachary's blankets and listened to him murmur in his sleep. Then in a quick movement, I slid into the bed next to him. He jerked awake, and I put my hand over his mouth. "You listen to me," I said, and something in my tone made him stop struggling. "I'm going to tell everyone you deliberately took my blankets as an excuse for us to share a bed together, that you told me if I didn't get in your bed with you, you'd make up some story about catching me in the bathroom jacking off." He started struggling again but didn't make any noise. That fact alone told me I'd won. With my free hand, I grabbed his right hand and squeezed as hard as I could, crushing his fingers, the way he always did when he shook hands. He stopped struggling.

"Your other option," I whispered, "is to go sleep in my bed tonight in just your garments with only that flimsy sheet for cover. I'll sleep in your bed with the warm blankets and tell everyone you made this exchange as a sacrifice because you're such a great guy." I gently removed my hand from his face.

"It's fifty degrees in here."

"Use Celsius, please."

"I'll tell the president. He'll believe me."

"Maybe he will, and maybe he won't. But you'll never make Assistant to the President, will you? He'll always doubt you just a little."

There was silence for a long moment, and then Elder Zachary hissed, "You're a bastard."

"I follow the example of my leaders," I replied, "as I've been taught to do." I felt a little sick as I realized that was probably true. What kind of jerk would do what I'd just done?

Elder Zachary climbed out of the bed quietly and softly walked off down the hall toward the nursery bedroom. I hated forcing my companion to share a room with this creep, and I knew the battle wasn't over, that Zachary was better at this than I was, that he'd find a way to take revenge. As I lay there listening to the junior zone leader's breathing from the cot on the other side of the room, I suddenly realized how ridiculous the whole scenario was.

Servants of the Lord?

Maybe Elder Burton was right and I should just head home and start the next portion of my life without looking back.

But I wanted to see if Dario would eventually join the Church. I wanted to see other people in this country join the Church. I wanted to be a part of the gospel growing here. It was true even if some of the members weren't perfect.

Even if none of us were.

I climbed out of the bed and pulled down the front of my garments. I pointed my penis at Zachary's bed and let loose a long stream of urine, aiming the trail up and down the length of the mattress, making sure the blankets were soaked as well.

Then I headed back for my room. I nudged Elder Zachary. "What?" he hissed.

"I'm sorry," I said. "I was wrong. You can go back to your own bed. I apologize."

He got up from the bed and put his face in mine. "You'll regret this, mister. Ti prometto." Then he hurried out of my room. As soon as he was in the hallway, I locked the door.

Then I walked over to Elder Burton's bed and shook him gently. He woke up groggily and sat up. "What is it?" he said.

"Do you mind if I get in bed with you?" I asked softly. "It's pretty cold in here."

"I—I was going to ask, but I thought you'd think it was too gay."

I slid in next to him. The cot was so narrow that the only way we could both easily fit was to spoon. I turned Elder Burton away from me and snuggled up into his back, putting one arm over his chest. "I'm going to tell you a story," I whispered into his ear.

At first, he gasped when I told him what I'd done, but soon we were both giggling uncontrollably. When we finally settled down several minutes later, I felt so warm inside that I had the best sleep I'd had in quite some time.

In the morning, Elder Burton and I headed to the kitchen together and shared the last of my Corn Flakes.

Elder Zachary had dark circles under his eyes, as if he'd spent the night sitting at his desk.

He never said a word.

Helping the Hookers

I was finally senior companion in my missionary district in Cincinnati, after eight months out in the field. Since sisters only served eighteen months, I was almost halfway finished, so I was relieved to no longer be a junior. I was staying in the same apartment, my senior was transferring to another zone, and my new junior was coming in her place. I was simply switching titles. While my departing companion was trusted to travel on her own, it was forbidden for me to stay by myself until the new sister arrived, so I had to hang out with two other sisters from another district for most of the day. When we finally received word that Sister Owens had arrived, the other two sisters drove me back to my apartment, and I let my new companion into the building. Sisters got to live in nicer buildings than the elders did, though not by much.

"Sister Buxton," Sister Owens gushed, "it's so nice to meet you." She was short, about 5'3", slightly plump, with short, blond hair and a big smile. I was a good three inches taller, with medium length brown hair, and a slimmer waist. Of course, I had a slimmer bosom as well, to my chagrin. "My first companion was great, but I've heard even better things about you. I can't wait for us to start teaching."

The fact was that teaching was a pretty rare event for most of us in the mission. The average baptism rate for sisters was 2.3 members over an entire mission. The elders had slightly higher numbers, but then, they served an extra six months in the field.

"Are you up for some action tonight?" I asked. "It's already past 5:00, and we have to be back home by 8:30." That was an hour earlier than the elders were allowed to stay out. "I can drive you around the area and give you an idea of what we have to work with."

"Oh, that sounds wonderful! Maybe we can spot someone who's just waiting to hear the gospel!"

Someone with an aura over their head, I knew she meant. "Maybe so."

I gave Sister Owens half an hour to unpack and unwind, and then we hopped in the car, still both wearing our Sunday best. Every day except Preparation Day when we did our chores required our Sunday best, so the term rather lost its meaning. Now that I was senior, I got to sit behind the steering wheel, and I smiled. It was a privilege to have a car, but in return we had to keep track of our mileage for the mission president, so joyriding as we were doing tonight was strictly frowned upon. Our area was rather poor, and my last companion had hated it. She'd come from an upper middle class home in Sandy. From the eager, naïve look on Sister Owens' face, I expected her background was somewhat similar. It wasn't very different from my own experience growing up in Orange County in southern California.

"Ooh. Thugs." Sister Owens pulled her arms over her chest as we passed a few young men walking down the sidewalk in T-shirts and sweat pants.

"I don't see any guns or knives," I pointed out.

"Hmm," was my companion's only response. This might be harder than I thought.

I drove past a playground where several other young men were playing basketball, and then through another depressed area. "Are you sure this is safe, Sister Buxton?"

"This is where the Lord has called us to serve," I replied.

"Ooh."

It might have been a moot point. If we didn't baptize anyone soon, the mission president said he might close our district altogether. It wasn't bringing in enough "quality" converts, he'd told me last week during our quarterly interview. I suspected he meant tithe-payers, but I suppose he could have meant almost anything. I had baptized one woman, a single mother, who'd gone almost immediately on Church welfare.

Naturally, I didn't baptize her myself. Sisters could only teach. It was the elders who did the baptizing.

I parked the car along the curb. "Why are we stopping?"

I pointed through the windshield.

"That woman?" asked Sister Owens.

I nodded.

"She looks a little worldly."

The woman was clearly a prostitute. As missionaries, we were only allowed to do four hours of "community service" a week. Any more would take too much time away from proselytizing. All my previous companions had ever wanted to do was shelve books at the library or babysit for some of the sisters in the ward. Not that giving mothers a break once in a while wasn't a good thing. But I'd been waiting for months to finally be able to do something a little more meaningful. And now that I was a senior, I was going to do it.

"Let's go talk to her," I said.

We climbed out of the car, and Sister Owens looked over her shoulder as we approached the woman. It was already dark out, and the streetlights didn't offer much illumination.

"Good evening," I said.

"I don't do threeways," the woman replied. She was thin and bony, with acne scars, and an olive complexion. Her dark hair looked as if it could have used one more comb through.

"We're missionaries with The Church of Jesus Christ of Latter-day Saints," I explained.

"Oh, brother."

"I just wanted to know what we could do to help you," I said. "Do you need us to get you some condoms? Or should we get you some pepper spray? I want to make sure you can defend yourself if you need to."

The woman cocked her head, but it was Sister Owens I was trying to ignore. Her hand flew to her mouth as she finally realized the situation.

I supposed the ideal action on my part would have been to offer the woman a good-paying job. But even our Ward Employment Specialist couldn't help most of the poorer ward members as it was. There really wasn't much I could do there.

"I've got plenty of condoms," the woman said.

"I'm Eileen." I offered my hand. It was against mission rules to use our first names, but I knew calling myself "Sister" would only alienate her further.

The woman looked at me suspiciously, and then looked dismissively at Sister Owens. But I kept my hand extended, and finally she took it. "Martha," she said, shaking her head in a shudder. "Ugh. Isn't that ugly?"

I smiled. "It's gotten a bad rap," I admitted, "but Eileen's no winner, either."

The woman smiled back. "You can't hang around here much longer. It drives away the customers."

"Well, that's a good thing, isn't it?" asked Sister Owens. She couldn't quite figure out what to do with her hands. Should she clasp them together? Keep them by her side? Keep brushing obsessively at her hair?

I turned to my companion. "Martha has to eat, you know."

Sister Owens frowned. "Do you...do you...like it?" she asked the woman. Now her hands were held out in front of her as if she planned to latch onto something.

"Are you for real?" Martha laughed.

"Is it ever romantic?" my companion persisted, and I closed my eyes in embarrassment. She must have been thinking of Richard Gere. Not that a good Mormon girl would have ever watched that movie to begin with. I'd obviously watched it, though. But no one like him ever came in this neighborhood, that was clear.

"I don't kiss," said Martha.

"Ohhh," said Sister Owens, nodding. "That must be how you keep from getting pregnant."

Martha stared at Sister Owens, then looked at me, and then looked at Sister Owens again.

"I don't want to take up too much of your time," I said. "But really, what can we do to help? Do you need anything? Even for us to stand half a block away and make sure no one roughs you up?"

Martha laughed. "And you could protect me?"

"Well, we have cell phones," I said.

"You girls go home and watch *Two Broke Girls* and keep your doors locked, and I'll be okay out here by myself. It's not like I don't have my pimp to protect me."

"Do you need us to protect you from him?"

"You girls go on home or he'll be here after *you*."

I began to realize that this effort on my part wasn't terribly different from the routine "help" we offered people by preaching. Most people didn't want that particular kind of help. And Martha didn't want any other kind of help we could offer, either.

What *did* people want, I wondered.

What did I want?

"You have any children you need us to babysit?" I asked, resorting to what I knew best.

Martha stared at us again. A car pulled up and someone rolled down the window. "Gotta work, girls." We turned to go. "But if you're serious about the babysitting, can you be here tomorrow morning at 7:00?"

I smiled. "We'll see you at in the morning," I said.

Martha didn't smile or nod or acknowledge us any further in any way. Instead, she leaned against the car and peered in through the window. I pulled Sister Owens away, and we headed back for our own car.

"7:00 is awfully early," she said as I opened her door. "We don't usually leave the apartment until 9:30."

"I'm thinking we may not do things the normal way for the next couple of months," I said. "Do you mind terribly?" This was going to be a real drag if she wasn't on board.

Sister Owens stood with her hand on the door handle, looking back up the street toward the other car. Its passenger door was just closing after Martha had climbed in. "It may be too late to help that woman," she said, "but her kids need all the positive influence we can bring. We can play educational games, teach them colors and numbers and how to read or whatever."

Or maybe we'd just give the woman a break, I thought. Somehow, now that seemed like a worthy goal.

"I'm not really sure how this will play out," I admitted. "I just want to try to help someone who truly needs it. Do something more than bake cookies for a sick member."

Bringing food to the sick was a good thing.

We sat in our seats, closed the doors, and I started the car. "Well, at least it'll give me something interesting to write home about," said Sister Owens, buckling up.

Yes, I thought, watching the car with Martha in it disappear around a corner. We still saw the poor and suffering as zoo animals, didn't we, an exhibit that could at best capture our attention for a few passing moments, make us feel we were part of a larger world, while remaining safely in our own. Wasn't that really part of the reason I was doing this? But I supposed that was better than not even seeing certain people as worthy of our attention at all. In any event, once the zone leaders got wind of what we were doing, they'd probably put a stop to it. But I still had ten months left. I was called to serve. And I was going to do more than measure my success by baptizing 2.3 people on my mission, 1.7 of whom would go inactive two months later.

Perhaps babysitting for a prostitute wasn't the answer, but I expected Martha would have some better ideas of her own if I asked her.

I would ask her in the morning.

Movie Night with the Missionaries

I've always loved movies. I remember as a child wanting to stay up late to watch a monster movie, but I was scared to do it by myself. I begged my mother to stay up with me. She refused, I pouted, and then she leaned over and whispered, "You can leave the lights on after the movie is over." I smiled and the deal was made.

I don't even remember what movie that was.

A few years later, my best friend Jeff and I used to stay up together to watch silent movies on PBS on Friday nights. Silent movies! What boy today would sit through that? Come to think of it, how many kids even in the early 1970's were willing to do such a thing? I just really liked movies.

Even though we were devout Mormons, I was still able to see some R-rated films. When *The Exorcist* came out, Jeff and I begged my mother to take us. She had no desire to see the movie herself but dutifully bought three tickets. Once past the ticket taker, she slipped into another theater and let Jeff and me go in to see the horror movie by ourselves. I believe we were twelve or thirteen at the time.

But Mormonism did have its effect on me, and when I was flying across the Atlantic to serve my mission in Portugal, I refused to watch the in-flight movie: *Fame*. It was not only rated R, but I'd also heard there was a gay character. I was not going to pollute myself with such filth while I was serving the Lord.

The same Puritanical streak remained after I returned a couple of years later and went back to college in Indiana. I did still love film and took two film classes, two in American film and one in foreign film. But I ended up walking out of the classroom one day when the teacher showed us a very sexual French movie.

I don't even remember what it was.

For a Single Adult activity at church, someone picked *Ladyhawke* for us to watch, and a young woman leaped in front of the screen at one point, spreading her arms wide to block the image, exclaiming, "There's a scene here where we almost see Michelle Pfeiffer's breasts."

It was the "almost" that got me. Maybe Mormons were overreacting a bit to all this stuff.

Still, I remember the next time we had Movie Night, and I was in charge of selecting the film. I picked *Rear Window*, a safe enough experience. There were still loud moans, though, when I announced what we'd be seeing. "An old movie?" someone complained. "It's going to be so boring." But it wasn't long before the others were on the edge of their seats, screaming in suspense.

That was when I recognized two things about myself—first, I liked movies most other people my age tended to ignore out of hand, and two, maybe I needed to go back to seeing rated R movies like I'd done as a kid. After all, I'd turned out all right, hadn't I?

You can imagine how that plan ended. Open-mindedness and Mormonism didn't mix very well. I was excommunicated for apostasy by the time I was twenty-seven. As cliché as it sounds, one could hardly watch *2001: A Space Odyssey* and not start to think.

I went on to get an English degree, then a Masters, and finally a PhD, with an emphasis in film as literature. Even with a doctorate, though, I ended up mostly teaching composition courses to college freshmen. But I did get to teach one film course each semester. We watched one film a week, and it was always frustrating trying to select the fifteen films most likely to be overlooked by the younger generation that were also "essentials" (a term I borrowed from Turner Classic Movies).

Perhaps that's too much background. But these were all things I was mulling over on a particularly rainy Wednesday night in Portland when I heard a knock on the door. My front door had a speak-easy window, so I opened it and looked out. There were two damp Mormon missionaries, both still in their teens from the looks of it.

"Yes?" I said, as if I didn't know who they were.

"Good evening!" said one of them, blond, with a perky smile and dimples. His nametag read "Elder Hunter." He gave his little spiel while the other missionary, Elder Craddock, looked on anxiously, his dark hair matted to his head. While it was past 7:30, there was still another ninety minutes before sundown. My front garden, full of purple and yellow iris, had to look inviting, even in the gloom.

I had no desire to listen to the missionaries, and no desire to torment them for their beliefs. I was about to politely turn them away when there was suddenly a break in the clouds, and a beam of sunshine fell directly on the front porch. It's not that I believed in signs. The sunlight simply made me feel good after a tough day on campus.

"I'll let you guys in for a few minutes," I said, "but we'll have to set up some ground rules."

They smiled happily, eager to accept pretty much any offer they received. I opened the door and guided them to the sofa. We all introduced ourselves, and then Elder Hunter whipped out his plastic-coated flip charts.

"Hold on," I said. "First of all, I'm an ex-Mormon." Their faces fell. "Secondly, I'm not the least bit interested in going back to the Church." The two young men looked at each other as if contemplating leaving right on the spot. "However," I continued, and the note of concession gained their interest again, "I'm willing to let you guys give me the discussions, just so you can up your weekly stats, but on one condition."

"What is it?" asked Elder Hunter. He looked both resigned and anxious.

"I'm a film teacher, and I know you guys are hopelessly out of touch with some of the country's best films. If you guys come over two nights a week for the next several weeks, I'll show you a movie of my choosing each evening, and then after the movie, you can teach me a lesson."

"We're not allowed to watch movies," said Elder Craddock.

Elder Hunter held up a hand to quiet his companion. "What's the catch? Are you going to show us porn?"

I laughed. "No, but there will be some rated R movies. You may as well know that up front."

"What movies do you want to show us?"

"No previews. You find out the night we see the movie, and you have to watch the whole thing if you want to teach me a lesson."

The two missionaries looked at each other, and then Elder Hunter leaned over to whisper something in Elder Craddock's ear, and Elder Craddock leaned over to whisper something back. It was a sweet deal. They got to break a suffocating mission rule "for the greater good," got to relax and enjoy their evening, and still got to score some stats for their weekly letter to the mission president. They would only reject such an offer if they were too closed-minded to reach in the first place.

Like I had been on my mission, I reflected.

"Before you make up your mind," I said, "I want to point out that I will *not* be cooking you dinner first. You'll come around 7:00, see a movie of my choosing, teach me a lesson of your choosing, and go home." I paused. "Oh, and no prayers and no testimonies. That kind of stuff drives me crazy."

The elders looked concerned about this latest development and whispered to each other another couple of minutes. Finally, though, they both turned back toward me, and Elder Hunter nodded. "It's a deal." He reached out to shake my hand, and I complied with his request. "Can we start tonight?" he went on. "Do you have any popcorn?"

I laughed. "These won't be popcorn kind of movies, I'm afraid." I was about to stand up and walk over to my DVD shelves when I had another thought. "I suppose we'd better decide first on the nights you're to come over. I expect you'll have a harder time making appointments on Friday and Saturday nights, when so many other people are busy. As it turns out, I'm recently widowed, so I'd appreciate not being alone on those nights. Plus, it'll be harder for you to get dinner appointments with the local members on Monday nights when they're doing their Family Home Evening, so if you're up to it, we'll upgrade to three nights a week, and you can come over Mondays, Fridays, and Saturdays, until you get transferred, or until you get tired of coming." Movies were an escape, and at this point in my life, I needed an escape as much as these young men did.

The missionaries looked at one another, nodded, and turned back to me.

"This week, we'll start tonight, and then you'll come back this Friday, Saturday, and next Monday, and so on. You'll run out of lessons before I run out of movies, but I'm sure you guys can figure something out to teach me, can't you?"

They smiled.

And over the next few seconds, I had to decide what film to show these young men tonight. Part of me wanted to show them the great classics I knew they'd never watch on their own, something like *Key Largo*, or *Shadow of a Doubt*, or *I Remember Mama*, or *The Miracle Worker*. Or even something like *To Sir, With Love* or *Wait Until Dark* or *The African Queen* or *Roman Holiday*. To open their minds to the great films from other countries was just too much to shoot for, but even limiting myself to American films was daunting. There were dozens and dozens of films these young men would never see, not only because of their age but also because of their religion. I had to pick out something that overcame both these obstacles.

I reached onto my shelves and pulled out a DVD. "Have you ever seen *The Accused* with Jodie Foster?"

"Never heard of it," admitted Elder Hunter. "What's it about?"

I paused. "I'm not going to tell you. There's definitely a certain enjoyment in anticipating something you know is coming," I said, "but there's another kind of enjoyment that comes from just experiencing something without any expectations. We'll go that route." Seemed a reasonable approach, since I had no idea what I was hoping to get out of my proposition in the first place. We'd all just play it by ear.

Elder Hunter shrugged, and I slipped the DVD into my player. Then I dimmed the lights, but not so much that the missionaries would feel uncomfortable. Still, there were a few shouts of "Oh, my heck!" and "Flip!" during the presentation. But for the most part, the guys watched in rapt silence. When the movie was over, I turned off the machine and raised the lights back up to normal.

"What did you think?" I asked.

"Oh, we don't have to talk about it now, too, do we?" asked Elder Hunter. "You only said we had to watch, and then we could teach you."

I chuckled. "Fair enough. I suppose it's your turn now."

Elder Hunter and Elder Craddock traded off portions of their first discussion, about Joseph Smith's vision of God the Father and Jesus Christ. I was sure they had no idea that there were multiple versions of that story by Joseph Smith himself, sometimes saying he saw angels, sometimes saying he saw God, sometimes saying he saw Jesus, sometimes saying he saw any combination of the above. I understood that memory wasn't perfect. Sometimes, I was sure a scene took place in a certain movie and then it turned out to be in a completely different one. Still, it seemed odd not to remember something as profound as whether or not you saw God. But I wasn't going to torment these young men. I'd made a deal and I was going to stick with it.

As agreed upon, the elders came back three times a week for the next several weeks. I knew they were enduring the movies just so they could teach, and they knew I was enduring the teaching just so I could share the movies. Both parties were sure that our side was going to win over the other. It was pathetic for me to realize that in essence I was acting just as immaturely as they were. But we kept up with the program anyway.

I showed the elders *Born into Brothels* next, followed by *Made in Dagenham*, to finish my ridiculously short course on feminism that I'd begun with the first movie. I thought about offering some comedy, as in many ways laughter was an even stronger teacher than sobriety, but I wanted the missionaries to be aware they were in class. I knew that they'd been told, "You're here to teach, not to be taught," and I wanted to be blatant that yes, I was deliberately trying to teach them. So next came another ridiculously short course, this one on race, as I showed them *Selma* and *Four Little Girls* and *Twelve Years a Slave*. Next came the Jewish week with *Fiddler on the Roof*, *Gentleman's Agreement*, and *Schindler's List*. The elders didn't even try to teach me a lesson after that last movie. They just shook my hand in silence and left to go back to their apartment in muted contemplation.

The following week I presented *Maurice*, *The Times of Harvey Milk*, and *The Imitation Game*. The elders were struggling to come up with even remotely meaningful lessons by this point. I couldn't resist pointing out the obvious. "If you guys have the greatest and most profound message the world has ever known, how come you have so little to say about it, while I still have plenty to say of my own?" I was afraid that might force them to cut off their visits to me, but I'd already infected their minds with at least a little knowledge, I felt, and no one could really take that away.

But the elders came back the next week, too. I showed them *An Inconvenient Truth* on Monday, *Going Clear: Scientology and the Prison of Belief* on Friday, and *This Film is Not Yet Rated*, that last one just to plant a seed that maybe they shouldn't be worrying about R ratings so much in the future. I had hoped to keep up the screenings another few weeks, perhaps even a few months. I knew sometimes missionaries stayed in the same district for a very long time. I suspected if either one of these guys was transferred, that would put an immediate stop to the visits. But that Saturday night after the credits rolled up, Elder Hunter cleared his throat.

"I appreciate what you've been trying to do," he said in a solemn voice, "but it's clear you're being led by the Adversary." He raised his hand to stop me from speaking, even though I hadn't made any attempt to do so. "I'm not saying you're deliberately evil. You're just deceived. We see it with people every day. We had hoped you'd feel the Spirit by our presence and eventually come around. But we see now your heart is simply too hardened." He then went on to bear his testimony, breaking our agreement, and his companion followed with a testimony of his own.

What was I going to do in return? Bear my testimony of the value of movies? Say "I know Audrey Hepburn is a true actress"? Proclaim, "I know that screenwriting is true"? It was definitely often truer than scripture, I thought, but then, that wasn't setting a very high bar.

I'd gambled on the human capacity for growth, and I'd lost. I didn't know why it surprised me. The same thing happened every semester with the majority of my students. And those were mostly non-religious people who actually believed in the power of storytelling to begin with. So what was I expecting?

"Well," I said as the elders stood up to leave, "I want to thank you for making the attempt to have an open mind. And you've certainly kept my own mind off my recent loss." I realized that in all these weeks, they hadn't asked a single question about my husband, didn't even know I'd had a husband and not a wife. I had to wonder about people who had so little curiosity regarding others. Maybe these guys wouldn't have been the greatest catch for my side, anyway.

I held out my hand, and then I had a thought. "How about one last deal?" I asked.

Elder Hunter looked at me suspiciously.

"If you guys come over for one more week of movies, I'll get baptized next Sunday."

"But it won't be real," protested Elder Craddock. Elder Hunter held up a hand to stop him.

"I would have thought you'd have shown your best movies first," said Elder Hunter, looking at me carefully. "You're not going to show us porn this time, are you?"

"No promises," I said. "And there's one more condition."

"Yes?"

"There will be *four* movies this week. You'll have to come over on Wednesday, too."

"Sounds like you're trying to brainwash us." Elder Hunter stared at his Book of Mormon and his flip charts for a long moment and then looked back at me. "Okay," he said. "But you have to promise not to leave the Church for a full year." He saw the expression on my face and continued quickly, "You don't have to *come* to church for a year, just stay a member."

Now I gave him an appraising look. "Deal," I said, and we shook hands.

As I watched the elders leave, I wondered why I'd made such an arrangement. The truth was that I'd been celibate the past six months, ever since David had died in a car accident. And I did want community again. Maybe church wouldn't be so bad. After all, I was perfectly capable of watching a comedy movie or science fiction film without believing it. I could enjoy church again, too.

And I wanted to see the elders again.

So I prayed that night for the first time in years, and I prepared my final onslaught of movies. On Monday, we watched *Bridegroom*. Wednesday was *Upstairs Inferno*. Friday was *Pride*, and Saturday was *The Short Bus*.

If these guys could let a fantasy guide their lives, there was no reason I couldn't indulge in a little wishful thinking, too, was there?

I'd already had to undergo the baptismal interview the day before in order for arrangements to be made for Sunday, and I'd lied my way through the questions about belief. Now the films were over, and the only thing left was for me to fulfill my part of the agreement the following day.

"Did you enjoy the movie?" I asked as I pulled the DVD from the player. I admit, it was a cruel question.

"We've got to get out of here!" said Elder Craddock. Elder Hunter held up a hand.

"Why did you show us that movie?" asked Elder Hunter.

I shrugged. "Because it's good," I said.

"You're trying to seduce me, aren't you?"

I had to laugh, thinking of Dustin Hoffman.

"I knew we shouldn't have agreed to those last four movies," he went on. "The Spirit testified to me that it was a mistake. But I wanted that baptism on my record. And now..."

"Yes?" I asked.

"Now I want to see more movies."

"Elder Hunter, are you crazy?"

Elder Hunter looked me in the eyes, and in an instant, we both *knew*.

"Can you guys come over tomorrow night?" I asked. "After the baptism?"

Elder Hunter shook his head, and I thought I'd lost again. "There's not going to be any baptism," he said, and his companion moaned. "But there's a movie I've wanted to see for a long time."

"What is it?" I asked.

"*Latter Days.*"

I nodded, and Elder Craddock looked like he was about to run away. I wasn't sure how much longer these movie nights would be able to go on, even with Elder Hunter's renewed interest. But then, I began to suspect that Elder Hunter might want to continue these visits, even if his companion was no longer willing to come along.

If I was a mentor, I couldn't truly be a boyfriend. But the relationship, whatever it turned out to be, would do for the time being, perhaps get us both through a rough patch.

"It just so happens I do have a copy of that film," I said, "and I've got a few others I think you might like, too."

Elder Craddock opened his mouth in horror, but Elder Hunter and I just looked at each other for the longest time, smiling. "I remember something you told us that first night," he said thoughtfully. I raised my eyebrows in response, and he continued. "There's a certain enjoyment in anticipating something you know is coming."

I laughed, and gave him the temple handshake as I showed him to the door.

Preaching While Black

"What a nice talk you gave, Elder Washington," said Sister Kyzar, shaking my hand languidly as we left the chapel.

"So civilized," added Sister Fowler, the bishop's wife, nodding in approval.

I wanted to say, "Were you expecting a lot of amens and hallelujahs?" but I just smiled and nodded back.

"And you're so articulate," Sister Kyzar continued.

Please, stop while you're ahead, I thought. Then I realized it was already too late for that. You'd think white people in McComb had never seen a black person before. This was my third area since arriving in the mission, and the reaction had been pretty much the same everywhere I went. I had experienced plenty of racism up in Queens where I was from, but there was an entirely different level down here in Mississippi.

Sacrament was the last meeting of our three-hour block, so my companion, Elder Cole, and I climbed in our car with the other two elders from our district, Andrews and Witherspoon. Andrews was the district leader. Missionaries often called the district leader's companion in every district the "district n—" because he always ended up doing most of the chores for the group that the district leader didn't want to do. One of the other elders would always let the term slip, then look worried that I'd take offense and say something like, "I didn't mean…" and look embarrassed.

What kind of things did they say when there wasn't a black person around at all?

My family had joined the Church when I was twelve, and even in New York, we were a small minority in the congregation. Down here, we were almost non-existent. There had been a black woman in my first congregation in Brookhaven, but when she played the organ, she threw in some "gospel" touches, and I could see the other ward members shaking their heads patronizingly. They'd say things like, "She hasn't fully converted yet, has she?" and other similar comments.

To be fair, though, they made the same remarks about a white convert from Catholicism who still crossed himself when he walked into the chapel.

Perhaps I was being overly sensitive.

It was my week to cook, and this being Sunday, I'd prepared most of the meal in the morning before services. Now all I had to do was bake the final product, and an hour later, lunch was served. The other three elders sat around the kitchen table, eager to eat.

"Lasagna?" asked Elder Andrews in amazement. "Wow. It smells great. How did you ever learn to cook Italian food?"

I shrugged. "I learned to read when I was five."

Andrews frowned but then was overwhelmed by the smell again and quickly offered a prayer so we could all begin eating. Everyone exclaimed in gratitude over the meal, and we discussed our current investigators as we ate. Andrews and Witherspoon were teaching two families. One was Baptist and the other was Methodist. Both were having difficulties accepting we were truly Christian. "I keep pointing to my nametag and saying 'It's The Church of Jesus Christ of Latter-day Saints! How can we not be Christian?'" Elder Andrews shook his head in disgust. "People are so ignorant here in the South."

"We're teaching a Jew," said Elder Cole. "He says there are so few members of his religion here they only meet a couple of times a year on holidays, so he'd like to join a group where he can participate more regularly."

"He can certainly do that as a Mormon," I agreed, smiling. Almost every member I knew held two or three jobs. We were practically forced to come to church every week. I wondered what the activity rate was for other religions where the members weren't "called" into servitude.

Elder Andrews looked thoughtful for a moment as he ate another bite of the lasagna. He glanced at his companion for a second and then turned to me. "I've heard of Ethiopian Jews," he said directly, "so I guess I see why you're teaching him, but shouldn't you really be focusing on your own people? Don't you think that's why the Lord sent you down here?"

I swallowed my own bite of lasagna as I tried to decide how to answer. "I am teaching my own people," I said carefully. "I'm teaching humans."

"You know what I meant."

Yes, I did.

To be clear, my family back home often asked me the same question. The Church needed more African-Americans, and it was my duty to recruit them. However, I found most blacks decidedly uninterested in joining. And I had my own prejudices to deal with. When Elder Cole and I talked to a black person, I would immediately start thinking, "What would the other members think of him? He's not speaking correctly. Oh, my Lord, he's eating watermelon! We'll find someone else."

The truth was that we didn't find many people of any race who were interested in the Church. I'd been out nine months and had yet to baptize my first convert.

Elder Cole washed the dishes after we finished eating, but I stayed in the kitchen to recite some memorized verses for him so we could count it as study time. "You have such a good memory," my companion said, shaking his head in wonder.

Why did I have to take everything as an insult? He would have said the same thing if I was white. I *was* smart.

The next few days passed uneventfully. It was now Elder Witherspoon's week to cook. He and Elder Andrews found a new golden contact on Tuesday, and Elder Cole and I taught a first discussion on Wednesday, but without a return appointment. On Thursday, my companion and I had dinner with a member family. I couldn't help but notice over the last several months that I was invited into members' homes a lot less often than other missionaries. I tried to chalk it up to the fact that the other companionship I was living with always included the district leader, who was usually more gregarious than I was. *Everything* didn't have to be about race.

Tonight, though, as we were eating fried chicken with rice and black-eyed peas, Sister Cunningham said casually, "It's so good to see a young man like you on a mission." There seemed to be a slight emphasis on the "you."

I stopped chewing.

"You must really be looking forward to turning white."

I stared at her. Was she making fun of the Church? Or was she serious? Elder Cole seemed to feel the latter, put his fork down with a clang, and almost shouted. "That's not what the Book of Mormon says! It was mistranslated! It says 'pure and delightsome'! It's 'pure and delightsome'!"

Sometimes, it was difficult dealing with the racist history of the Church. But we were getting better. You couldn't hate Germans today because of what happened seventy years in the past. You couldn't hate Italians because they had slaves two thousand years ago. I looked at Sister Cunningham, who had a slight smile on her face, almost a smirk. I realized that her comment hadn't been a simple accident.

Things had been different in Queens, and I kept reminding myself that not all Mormons were like this. Even here, most of the members were polite enough, almost painfully so, but polite was certainly a step forward for most of them. The Church said we learned "line upon line, precept on precept." It didn't seem to me that treating people as people was such a difficult concept, but it wasn't only Mormons who had trouble with that one.

Saturday, we got a call from one of the members. "I'm feeling really sick," said Brother Turner. "I need a blessing, but my Home Teacher isn't answering the phone. Is Elder Andrews in?"

"No, but Elder Cole and I can come over," I said. There was silence on the other end of the line, and I gritted my teeth. "I *do* hold the priesthood, you know."

"Oh, sure, sure!" said Brother Turner. "It's not that! It's just..."

"Yes?"

"It's...it's what the neighbors would think if they saw you come in." He paused for a brief second. "It's not that *I* mind, you see. But my kids have to play with the other kids around here. You understand."

"Well, I sure hope you feel better soon," I said and hung up. Then I felt like an ass. He couldn't help the culture he lived in.

Could he?

Tomorrow was Fast Sunday, so lunch today was the last food we'd eat until we returned from church the following day. The two sister missionaries had invited all four of the elders over to break the fast at their apartment on the other side of town. We could only go in their apartment if we left the door open, to prove we weren't all inside having sex. I usually devoted my fasts to asking for inspiration finding prospective converts. Of course, none of those fasts had worked out very well. This time, I was fasting for more patience and understanding as I dealt with outdated attitudes.

Then as I knelt beside my bed to pray just before lights out, I realized I was fasting for the wrong thing. "Heavenly Father," I prayed silently, "please help *other* people to understand." I climbed in bed, but a few minutes later, I was back on my knees. "No, I can only change myself," I prayed. "Help *me*."

Five minutes after that, my knees were on the tile floor again. "I'm here to help others change," I corrected myself. "Please help me change other people."

"For pity's sake," said Elder Cole from across the room. "Go to sleep already."

Fast and Testimony meeting was excruciating, as usual. That had been true even in New York. As people slowly talked about the most inane things, forcing some kind of epiphany into the discussion, I kept hearing my stomach growl. I looked about at the others sitting near me. They were all thinking about the gospel. I could only think about how people saw my color. I shouldn't be thinking about race all the time, I thought. I should be thinking about Christ. While I couldn't control the actions of other people, I could learn to control my own. I was in charge of my personal spiritual welfare, regardless of the lack of enlightenment of others. I had to stop letting myself be distracted. I was on a mission not only to teach others, but to grow in my own right.

After services, the sisters reminded us to come over for lunch and then drove off, but there was a baptismal service a half hour after Fast and Testimony meeting, so we elders stayed at church a little longer. It was merely a young girl who had turned eight, not a convert, but we needed to see baptismal clothes any time we had the chance, simply to be able to keep believing in the possibility. Why anyone would schedule a baptism on Fast Sunday, I didn't know, but eventually, we were on our way across town.

First, we were delayed by an accident. Then our tire went flat.

"Dagnabbit!" said Elder Andrews, pulling over. We all stepped out of the car and looked at the offending tire. "Elder Witherspoon and Elder Washington, will you two change that for us?"

The two junior companions. Or was it because we were the "district n—" and the real n—? It was infuriating never to know anyone's true motives. I nodded and helped Elder Witherspoon. Fifteen minutes later, we were on our way again, but I was in a decidedly foul mood by this point.

Probably just my blood sugar.

My attitude didn't improve when we arrived and discovered the sisters had apparently grown tired of waiting for us and were no longer in the apartment. "Flip!" said Elder Andrews. "I'm starving! They promised!"

"I'll bet there's still plenty of food in there," said Elder Cole. "You're the district leader. Don't you have a key to their apartment?"

Elder Andrews rubbed his chin. "Yes, but I didn't bring it. Didn't think I'd need it." He tried to turn the handle, but the door wouldn't budge. "Flip!" he said again. He tried calling on his cell and then looked disgusted. "They're not answering. Probably wouldn't come back for us anyway, if they were so anxious to leave."

"There's a McDonalds a few blocks away," I suggested.

"We can't buy anything on Sunday!" Elder Cole protested.

"I'm hungry," said Elder Witherspoon.

We all stood staring at the door another moment, and then Elder Andrews snapped his fingers. "I know! We'll break in. Elder Washington, go around and see if you can get in one of the windows."

Because I looked like I'd know how to break into buildings, I thought. I looked at Elder Andrews a long moment and was so hungry I actually considered his suggestion, but then I thought that with my luck, someone would report me, the police would come, and I'd end up on the news, one way or another.

And the worst part would be that all the members would look at each other afterward and nod knowingly.

"Do it yourself," I said.

Elder Andrews put his hands on his hips. "You remember the parable about the talents, don't you?" he asked.

"Yes?"

"As your priesthood leader, I'm ordering you to get us in that apartment."

My heart started beating faster, and I wanted to punch him right in the nose. I'd heard about "lying for the Lord." Was he now proposing "breaking and entering for the Lord"? I should tell the guy exactly what I thought of him. Did being a model Mormon missionary mean following orders, or did it mean *not* doing so? I was responsible for my own actions, no matter what pressure my peers put on me. What I wasn't going to do was allow the failings of others make me less than I was.

What would Martin Luther King do, I wondered? What would Joseph Smith do?

Then I remembered to ask the right question: what would Jesus do?

And then even that question didn't feel like the right one. It was simply a matter of what *I* wanted to do.

I breathed slowly and deeply for a moment as the other elders watched to see who was going to win the argument. It really should be neither of us, I decided.

"You guys can stand here and wait for the sisters to come back," I said, "or you can come with me for hamburgers and fries." I started walking off down the sidewalk. "My treat."

I walked a good twenty feet and thought I'd end up being reported to the president for abandoning my companion, but a few moments later, I heard quick footsteps as the others came to join me. "Really, Elder Washington? You're paying?" asked Elder Witherspoon. "You're such a cool elder." He paused. "And it's so nice to see a person like you with money."

Latter-day Leather

"I'm bored," said Elder Carlson, tapping the kitchen table with his index finger.

I closed my eyes in resignation. We'd been together over two months now, and my companion had begun saying this every few days the last couple of weeks. It was never a good sign. The first time he said it, he'd insisted we interrupt a drug deal near our Mid-City apartment, to call the participants to repentance. We were lucky all they did was give us the finger. The next time he said it, we'd tapped on the window of a rocking car late one evening on our way home. I can attest that interrupting a young couple having sex is not an effective way to introduce someone to the gospel. And finally, the last time he'd said, "I'm bored," he'd knocked on the door of a rectory and challenged a Catholic priest to baptism.

That wasn't very effective, either.

"Can't we just go tracting?" I asked, picking up my plate and carrying it to the sink. We'd had cheese sandwiches with pickle relish for lunch.

"We're in New Orleans," Elder Carlson countered. "Elder Mitchell, this is the chance of a lifetime. We could have been sent to Waco, Texas, you know. We need to take advantage of what we have." My companion was from Tooele, and I was from San Jose.

"We're here to talk to New Orleanians," I replied, "not crash jazz funerals for excitement."

"Elder Mitchell," Elder Carlson said quietly, "I've been out nineteen months. In all that time, you're the best companion I've ever had. We've never had a Companion Inventory that was unpleasant. You've only been out six months. You don't realize how rare that is. We have something special." He smiled. "Don't you want to create memories you'll have for the rest of your life?"

Elder Carlson was my second companion since the Missionary Training Center, and even though I only had my trainer to compare him to, I still knew that what he was saying was true. That last companion, a district leader, had forced me to stand on one leg as I recited my missionary discussions. Rules allowed me two months to memorize them all, but he felt that making the task more miserable would force me to learn more quickly, to get it over with. It worked, I suppose, but my most profound memory wasn't of the discussions. It was of how much I disliked him.

Elder Carlson, at least, was fun to be around. Most of the time.

On Preparation Day, we dressed in our civvies and jogged along Bayou St. John with the other runners, quoting scriptures back and forth to try to impress them. It hadn't worked, but it had been entertaining to us if to no one else. We'd even taken to memorizing completely obscure verses just to tease one another.

When we did our grocery shopping on Broad, we always made a point of buying a few navel oranges and bringing them to the old man who lived around the corner from us. Alfonso had confessed to being gay and enjoying our company. An old black man who had been poor and uneducated his entire life, he pointed out the teeth he was missing from the times he'd been beaten up as a young man for his proclivities. "You guys treat me right," he said once, smelling an orange. "The way church people should."

"Why don't you call him to repentance, too?" I asked Elder Carlson one day. "You do it to everyone else."

It had taken my companion a long moment before he responded. "That man has suffered enough. Heavenly Father is going to bless him in the next life, not punish him."

It was a decidedly un-Mormon response, but I found I liked it. Elder Carlson wasn't a bad guy.

My companion had taken to washing my feet once a week, to show his humility. I felt uncomfortable at first but eventually began enjoying the interaction. He bought me an Italian pastry on South Carrollton for my birthday. And he feigned illness one Sunday when I was in a bad mood, so we wouldn't have to go to church.

The least I could do was indulge him once in a while when he developed these whims.

"So what did you have in mind to decrease your boredom?" I asked. I kept remembering the saying, "Idle hands are the Devil's workshop." I liked staying busy. It kept me from thinking too much. Even doing something as dumb as the other things Elder Carlson had suggested would at least keep us occupied.

My companion gave me an appraising look. He tapped the table for another few seconds and then rubbed his chin. "We should go to the French Quarter," he said.

My mouth fell open. "The French Quarter is completely forbidden," I pointed out. "The mission president says not to go there under any circumstances."

Elder Carlson made a face. "Do you really think I'm going to get drunk?" he said. "Or go to a strip club?"

"Well, who else did you want to call to repentance besides drunks and strippers?"

"I don't know," he admitted. "I just feel the Spirit directing us to go there. We can walk around and play it by ear."

I'd heard of elders being sent home after a trip to the Quarter. One elder had been shipped back to Utah simply for sneaking out alone to see a PG-rated movie. A sister had been sent home for taking a sip of her investigator's champagne on New Year's. "I don't think it's a good idea," I said.

"My cousin spent two years in Italy," said Elder Carlson. "He was in Naples for six months and was never allowed to go to Pompeii. This guy in my ward went to Paris. And he couldn't go to the Moulin Rouge. One of the young women in my stake went to Hawaii, and she was never allowed to go to the beach."

"We're not tourists," I pointed out. "We're missionaries."

"I'm going to the French Quarter," Elder Carlson said firmly. "You can come with me or you can stay in the apartment. Your choice."

He was being unfair, and that made me angry. But if we were in danger for going into such a sin zone as a companionship, I knew he was in even greater danger going alone. He'd be sent home for sure. At least if we went together, we had a chance.

"You flipper," I said.

Elder Carlson smiled.

It wasn't P-Day, so we wore our white shirts and ties. We caught the streetcar down Canal Street and jumped off at the last stop by the casino. I didn't have a good feeling about this. My companion led the way, and once we passed the first block of buildings, we were officially in the French Quarter. I had to admit, it didn't look as scary as I'd expected. There was a used book store with perfectly normal people walking in and out. Nearby was a vinyl record store. A guy with long hair came out the door, but it wasn't as if he was smoking pot or anything.

We roamed up and down the streets, taking in all the sights. Lots of antique dealers with some beautiful old furniture and artwork. Several restaurants. Some apartments. A dress shop. A park with flowers. A police station. A fire department. A courthouse.

Some bars. And some drunks, even at this early hour. It wasn't even 2:30 yet.

Elder Carlson made no attempt to talk to anyone, and that was fine with me. I was actually growing a little tired of telling others they were living in sin and needed to change their lives. I had my own dark secrets, and I'd found that calling others to repentance did nothing to improve my own soul.

We passed a wax museum, a community theater, a store featuring homemade quilts, and a shop selling wooden toys. Around 3:30, Elder Carlson smiled and pointed to a large, open-air eating space, packed with people. "The Café du Monde," he said.

"We're not having coffee," I insisted. "I've got to draw the line somewhere."

"I'm sure they serve milk, too," he replied with a shrug. "I want a beignet."

We sat at one of the tiny tables, and soon a young Asian woman came to take our order. A few moments later, we were eating warm, square doughnuts covered in powdered sugar, and sipping our milk. Elder Carlson certainly irritated me at times, but there was no denying he was a fun guy to be around. I hoped we were able to stay together another month or two. Too bad I couldn't write home about any of this.

Just one more secret to keep.

I hoped we wouldn't be sent home.

Elder Carlson stopped eating. "Why the gloomy look?" he demanded.

I sighed. "Just thinking depraved thoughts."

He laughed. "You don't really ever have depraved thoughts, do you?" He took another bite. Some sugar dusted his tie.

I nodded. "Sometimes, I do." I looked about me at the others sipping their coffee at adjoining tables. "Even as close as you and I are, there are things I can't tell you." I took another swig of milk. I'd felt we were bonding a few moments ago. Now I felt more alone than ever. "We'd probably better finish up here soon and get back to work."

Elder Carlson frowned and finished his last doughnut. We left a small tip and walked back onto the street. But he wasn't heading back to Canal, toward the streetcar. He was heading the other way.

He sure could be annoying sometimes.

We passed a shop selling pralines, another dress shop, and a store selling Christmas ornaments. There was an Italian deli, and another bar. Then Elder Carlson stopped and pointed. He was smiling triumphantly.

"You can't be serious," I said.

"Let's go in."

"Elder, I *don't* want to be sent home."

"Who's going to know? You think the bishop is in there and will report us?"

"There are other members with secrets, too," I said.

He clapped me on the back and headed for the store. I shook my head and followed.

I was thoroughly mortified as we walked through the door, realizing we were both still wearing our nametags. It seemed dishonest to remove them at this point, so I just walked behind my companion, afraid even to pray for help. There were several other people in the store, all looking perfectly normal. Perhaps you couldn't trust anyone.

There were leather vests displayed, and leather pants, and leather armbands, and spiked bras, and whips, and boots, and leather caps, and all sorts of other things I didn't recognize. There were playing cards with naked women, and playing cards with naked men, a magazine rack of appalling images, a sign pointing to a tattoo and piercing parlor upstairs, and rows of rubber penises. Another sign pointed to DVDs in the back.

"Elder Carlson, we have to get out of here."

"Oh, my heck," he breathed. "Look at that!" He pointed to a photo on the wall. The place was filled with photos, of dominatrix women, of men exposing their behinds through holes cut out in their leather pants, of a man whose face was tightly covered in a leather mask, of someone strapped to a wooden X. But the photo my companion was looking at showed a man licking another man's boot.

He *liked* that?

My world was falling apart. We were missionaries. We were here to serve God. And it looked like we *both* had terrible secrets that were going to destroy us.

That was why places like this were off limits. Even staying in safe areas and spending our days doing the Lord's work, temptation was often too hard to resist. It was pure folly to walk this close to the edge. It was right to forbid missionaries to see Pompeii.

"We've got to get out of here," I repeated. I took my companion's arm and led him out to the street. He didn't resist but permitted me to lead him all the way back to the streetcar. We climbed on board, paid our fare, and sat down. Elder Carlson didn't say a word, staring out the window the whole time. When we reached Mid-City, I grabbed his arm again and guided him off the streetcar. We walked back to our apartment in silence.

It wasn't like Elder Carlson to be this quiet. He must be really shaken up. That wasn't good.

I started singing "Ye Elders of Israel." It was one of my companion's favorite hymns. He looked at me and frowned. I stopped singing.

Once inside the apartment, we sat down at the kitchen table. Elder Carlson stared at a scratch in the tabletop.

"You okay?" I asked. "Want me to fix something to eat? It's almost 5:00."

"I'm not hungry."

"Want me to read an *Ensign* to you? We're short on Companion Study this week."

He shook his head. I watched him sitting there, looking utterly miserable. I wasn't going to report this to anyone, though, and hopefully, he wouldn't, either. We wouldn't be sent home. We'd go back out and preach the gospel. We'd baptize someone. We'd have good missions. We'd get through this.

We sat in silence for more than an hour. I wanted to read the scriptures, but somehow I felt that not devoting my full attention to my companion would be an abandonment of some kind. So we just sat there.

Finally, after I was almost ready to scream, Elder Carlson spoke up. "Take off your shoes and socks," he said. "I need to wash your feet again."

"Elder…"

"I need to do this."

I nodded. We stood up and walked to the bathroom. I sat on the closed toilet lid while my companion kneeled in front of me. He filled a small plastic tub with warm water and gently put my feet into it. Grabbing a washcloth, he softly rubbed my feet. He seemed to be crying. My heart felt as if it would stop beating.

After about ten minutes, Elder Carlson grabbed a towel and dried my feet. But he stayed kneeling on the floor in front of me. I was just about to say something when he lifted my left foot.

"Elder..."

He leaned down and licked my toes.

"Oh, Elder!" I said. I didn't know what to do. I let him lick my feet for the next minute or two, feeling emotions I'd never felt before. And then I couldn't hold myself back any longer. The demons had been released. Only they didn't feel like demons. I grabbed my companion's shirt and pulled him roughly up to my face. I looked into his eyes, which looked directly back into mine. Then I kissed for the first time in my life.

And I knew what it was like to see Pompeii.

Splitting

Tanny peeked through the curtain to look at the two sister missionaries getting out of their car. They didn't seem happy to be there. She could hear them talking to each other. "Do we have to bring her along? She's so fat."

"She's weak. She needs us."

Tanny let the curtain fall back into place. The sister missionaries had only asked her to go on splits with them out of pity, not because they wanted her. She'd show them. When they went to teach someone, she would bear her testimony and bring down the Holy Ghost upon everyone. Then they'd see.

The chimes rang, and Tanny went over to open the door. "Hi, Sister Archer," she said sweetly. "Hi, Sister Blackburn."

"Good morning, Tanny. It's so good to see you." Sister Archer smiled beautifully. She was so pretty. Flawless skin. She looked like a saint. Tanny giggled. She *was* one.

"Did you need to come in, or shall we start working right away?"

Sister Archer laughed melodically. "Are you sure you want to work all morning? It must be so nice to be retired and not *have* to work."

"I'm not really retired," Tanny reminded her. "I'm disabled. It's not exactly the same thing. I'm only fifty-one." The sisters must both be around twenty, Tanny thought. To them, fifty-one probably sounded ancient.

"You're not *really* sick," said Sister Blackburn. "No one who lives the gospel is ever truly mentally ill." The bishop had told her the same thing. So had the Relief Society president. To her face. With real voices.

"Schizophrenia is a genuine disease," Tanny replied flatly. She remembered losing her friends over the years one by one after all her accusations. She remembered how her non-member family no longer talked to her. She remembered all the times she'd been called in by HR on her various jobs and fired.

Sister Archer laughed sweetly. "Well, you seem perfectly fine to me. Let's get going."

Tanny wasn't going to argue about it. Life these past three years since she'd finally been diagnosed and prescribed meds had changed dramatically for the better. Instead of hearing voices constantly, she could actually cope most days. She still heard them, of course, but not as frequently as before, though she continued to have bad days once in a while. She could still have worked part-time if she wanted to, almost certainly able to keep a job now that her auditory hallucinations were mostly under control. She just didn't see the point when Disability paid enough for this tiny apartment and food to eat, even if sometimes it was only a can of tuna. She had a DVD player and checked movies out of the library since she couldn't afford cable. But books were free at the library, too. Being poor was infinitely better than being ill. She was pretty content most of the time.

Except when she was unhappy.

"Who else is working with us this morning?" asked Tanny. "Veronica?" Veronica was another older single woman in the Relief Society.

"No. That fell through," said Sister Archer. "It's just us."

"But I thought the whole point of going on splits was to double the workload. I go out with one of you and someone else goes out with the other."

"It's just us," Sister Archer repeated.

The two sister missionaries stole glances at one another, and Tanny knew exactly what they were thinking. It was almost as if she could hear them. They were both afraid to be alone with her.

"We're going to see Sister Bounds," said Sister Archer. "She's feeling ill and needs someone to lift her spirits."

"She has a real illness," Sister Blackburn pointed out.

"Are we wearing masks?" asked Tanny. It was all fine and good to knock on someone's door and hand them a pie and then run off, but to deliberately spend time with the sick? Who would do such a thing on purpose?

"We're missionaries," said Sister Archer, not really answering Tanny's question. "We help those in need."

They were driving along the road, stopping at stoplights, passing stores. Tanny luxuriated in the feel of the air conditioning, of the freedom and comfort. She always had to ride the bus when going somewhere by herself. It must be wonderful to be a missionary, she thought. She leaned against the back seat to enjoy the ride, but she could see the two sisters in the front talking softly to each other.

"If she acts all weird in public, we're going to have to dump her on the side of the road," Sister Blackburn whispered.

"We can always call the elders to take her home."

"Elders can't be alone with women."

"Who would ever be tempted by *her*?"

Tanny looked out the window at some children playing on a playground.

Soon they were pulling up in front of a beautiful, two-story brick home in a lovely neighborhood. The lawn was immaculately manicured, with blooming camellias along the front of the house. They all climbed out of the car and walked up to the magnificent front door, made of dark, rich wood and beveled glass. Sister Archer knocked. A few moments later, the door opened and Sister Bounds stood there, looking pretty awful without her make-up. "Who invited her?" she whispered to the sister missionaries.

They went inside and asked Sister Bounds what she wanted for dinner, and then Tanny and the missionaries got to work in the kitchen preparing the meal. Tanny couldn't even imagine what it must be like to have such a large kitchen, with so much food in the refrigerator and pantry. The family even had their Year's Supply, while Tanny would have starved to death two weeks into the Apocalypse. She saw Sister Bounds eyeing her suspiciously, as if Tanny were going to sneak a ham into her blouse.

"What's your favorite meal, Tanny?" asked Sister Archer as they cooked.

"I like Salisbury steak," she replied.

"Huh?"

"Frozen dinners. They're my favorite thing. So easy."

"I see."

There was a lull in the conversation after that, but a while later, Sister Archer tried again. "Have you read any good books lately?"

"Jonathan Kellerman is my favorite author," said Tanny. Once she found a writer she liked, she went through every book he ever wrote.

"What does he write about?" asked Sister Archer.

"Murder and mayhem."

There was another long lull after that.

Tanny didn't really mind the silences. Sometimes, silence was better than sound. Sounds haunted her. Even with the meds. It was just nice to be spending time with someone. She didn't really have friends at church, hadn't since her Young Adult days. Even the Visiting Teachers never came by. The missionaries, though, they made an effort.

It was probably because they had nothing better to do, she realized. It was either stop by Tanny's apartment or go looking for converts. With those choices, even Tanny looked good.

They continued with the meal.

Finally, they were done, and Sister Blackburn went to tell Sister Bounds they were leaving. Then the three of them climbed back into the car. Tanny listened as they pulled away from the curb. "She said never to bring her back to her house," Sister Blackburn whispered.

"We're almost through. Hang in there a little longer." Then, looking brightly into the rear view mirror, Sister Archer smiled and spoke up more loudly. "Is there anywhere you'd like us to take you before we head back to your place?"

"No. Back home is fine." She wanted to go to the grocery and buy all the heavy items so she wouldn't have to carry them on the bus. She wanted to go to the park and look at all the flowers. She wanted to go to a museum, but who could afford that?

She wanted to go to another group therapy session. That sometimes almost felt like Single Adult Family Home Evening at church all those years ago.

They drove along in silence, but Tanny could still see the sisters looking at each other anxiously.

If only they held the priesthood, she thought. She could ask them to cast out the evil spirit inside her. She felt as if she were two people, a normal, happy woman, and an ugly, unpleasant freak everyone hated. How could that really all just be brain chemistry? Couldn't Heavenly Father get rid of the ugly part of herself no one liked? Why couldn't she be healed? What was the point of priesthood if it couldn't do anything?

She remembered reporting back to her doctor a few weeks after first going on medication. "It's a miracle!" she'd exclaimed.

"No," her doctor had replied. "It's science."

But it was a miracle she had found the science, Tanny had thought, though she kept that idea to herself. Then she'd seen the doctor turn to a nurse and whisper, "She's still delusional." And all her doubts and insecurities came flooding back.

If Heavenly Father couldn't cure her himself, why couldn't he at least let the doctors do it?

"I see my psychiatrist on Tuesday," Tanny announced. There was no response. "Every couple of months I have to go in and have my meds adjusted. Seems they're never quite right. I still hear the voices."

The two sisters looked at each other in the front seat.

Tanny laughed. "You'd die if you knew what words they were putting in your mouths." She chuckled again. "But I know enough now to realize what I hear isn't real." She paused. "Still, it's terrible to hear it. I'm never really quite sure what's real and what isn't. You could say something awful right to my face and then deny it and I'd never know the difference." She laughed again.

Sister Archer pulled into a Dairy Queen. "Why are we stopping here?" asked Sister Blackburn.

"Tanny, how would you like a great big strawberry shake?" Sister Archer asked, twisting her head to look into the back seat. "Or a banana split?"

"Oh, I'm already so fat."

"If you hear mean voices all the time, don't let yours be another of those voices. Tell yourself something nice." She smiled. "Let's go get some ice cream."

Tanny suddenly felt more alone than she'd ever felt. It was like being trapped in a cave-in, just barely able to hear sounds on the other side of the rocks, but knowing your rescuers would never reach you in time.

They stepped out of the car and walked into the restaurant. It was so cool and fresh and clean inside. They stood in line and looked up at the menu on the wall. Such a luxury to eat out, thought Tanny. Should she be wasting the missionaries' money? They needed that money to serve the Lord.

Sister Archer leaned over and whispered into Tanny's ear. "Get a large," she said. Then she turned to Sister Blackburn and laughed. "A large shake for a large girl!"

They picked up their order and then sat at a table to enjoy their ice cream.

Senior Discount

"So, Sister Penderly," I said into the phone, "do you think you'll be able to come to church this Sunday?" Sister Penderly was an inactive member, married to a non-member, whose kids were now grown and all living in sin. But I thought there was hope for her personally. No reason to condemn her to the Telestial Kingdom just because her family wasn't valiant. We preferred saving entire families, of course, but sometimes, individuals were important, too. Sister Penderly knew how to crochet. She'd be great in Relief Society.

"I don't know," the woman said hesitantly. "Bill might take the car on Sunday."

I closed my eyes. Always some excuse. You were never going to get to the Celestial Kingdom if you kept making excuses. "What if we come pick you up?" I asked.

There was silence on the other end of the phone. Then a sigh. "I suppose so. Thanks."

I put a smile in my voice. "We'll see you Sunday morning." I hung up the phone. Carl and I had been out on our couples mission for just over a year now and had five months left. I'd never gone as a young woman, though Carl had served two years in Canada. Now we were serving in the suburbs of Chicago. It was a dream come true. But it was sure a lot harder than I'd expected.

The first blow had come when I realized we were being called to reactivate inactive members, rather than bring new souls to the Church. There was something exciting about fresh blood. But the mission president had set other goals for us. "The Church is facing a serious problem with inactivity," he explained. "It's every bit as important to keep the Mormons who are already baptized temple-worthy as it is to bring new people in."

The second blow came in discovering how few inactive members wanted to be reactivated. And even when we did get an occasional member to start attending erratically again, we received no credit, the way the young elders got notches on their belts for baptisms.

"This is such a thankless job," I said, looking up from the phone at Carl's downcast face. He was sitting on the sofa reading the Doctrine and Covenants.

"You think Mormon had a rewarding job?" he asked, not even looking up. "He didn't have a single convert."

"He had Moroni," I pointed out.

"Well, Linda, we have our own children, too. And grandchildren."

"That reminds me. Valerie said she had a big announcement. I'd better check in."

"Probably pregnant again. Jobeth is almost three years old now."

"I wish we could go home and visit on the holidays," I said softly.

Carl chuckled. "We're setting them a good example. They feel our presence even when we're not there." He still hadn't looked up from the scriptures.

"I wish we were allowed to call," I went on. "Email seems so impersonal."

"At least we missed the Terrible Twos."

As seniors, we were allowed the use of our own laptop and didn't have to rely only on computer time at the library, though the mission was thinking of issuing iPads to the younger missionaries soon, too. The leaders were inspired in their use of technology. It was great having a living prophet. But we could only use the accounts set up by the Church, and all activity on the device was monitored. I wrote my daughter Susan every Preparation Day, and my grandchildren Valerie and David. Valerie had married at eighteen but David was still single.

Our son, Richard, had been killed on his mission. He'd been hit by a car while riding his bicycle. Our stake president had told us last year that the Lord wanted Carl and me to finish our son's mission for him. So Carl retired from work a couple of years earlier than planned. We sent in our papers.

And here we were.

I opened the laptop and composed a letter to Susan, CCing Valerie and David. "The work is going wonderfully," I began. "We've been working with one of the members for several weeks, and she has finally agreed to come to church again. The Lord loves all his children, even the ones who have gone astray. It's beautiful to see that Heavenly Father never forgets us, even if we forget him. We feel the Spirit every day as we do the Lord's work.

"Even at the grocery store, we get to serve the Lord. When I asked the girl at the register if I could get a senior discount, she looked at my driver's license and said I wasn't quite old enough. Then I showed her my nametag and asked if I could get a missionary discount. I knew I couldn't, but it led to a short discussion about the Church. I have to admit, sometimes I feel the Holy Ghost more when I'm talking to non-members, but it's just wonderful to focus on the gospel every minute of every day.

"How are you doing?"

I didn't write about my doubts. The mission president told us that it was important to let everyone back home feel the Spirit through our letters. That was a form of missionary work, too.

I missed talking about *The Voice*. And my latest cross stitch project. I didn't get to do any cross stitching out here.

I checked my inbox, but there were no new messages. The kids would all write later. They wrote almost every week. Well, Susan did, anyway.

I looked at Carl, still reading from his triple combination. "It's P-Day, Carl. Let's do something fun."

Carl lowered his book slightly and looked me in the eyes for a moment. "There's nothing more fun than reading the word of God." His eyes returned to the book.

I looked out the window. It was a beautiful day. I wanted to walk along the lake. I wanted to go to the park and play chess. I wanted to drive to the mall and see a movie, though there was probably nothing showing which was appropriate for Mormons at all, much less missionaries. I'd thought being a missionary would make me feel special. But mostly, I just felt frustrated. Or bored. Sometimes, I simply wanted to be a regular person again. I needed something to put me back in the proselytizing mood.

Maybe I should kneel beside my bed and pray for forgiveness. Clearly, there was something lacking in me.

I checked my inbox again, but there was still nothing.

I wanted to stay near Carl, so I leaned back on the sofa and napped. I used to ask him to read out loud to me so that we would at least be doing something together, but I found that was somehow worse than feeling alone, so now I let him read by himself. While dozing, I fantasized about Sister Penderly going back to church and becoming such a spiritual giant that she ended up bringing her husband and her kids to the gospel. Then I fantasized about her bringing her sister and her sister's family in, too. Then her neighbors. Reactivation could still be real missionary work. What I was doing was important, I told myself. These were the Last Days.

Just last night, I'd written in my mission journal how happy I was to serve, despite the president's restrictions. "The grandness of the missionary program is just one more proof that the Church is true." There were maybe 85,000 Mormon missionaries serving around the world now, bringing in two to three hundred thousand converts a year. That must be a billion dollars or more in free labor. Plus, as seniors, we were still paying tithing because we also had our pension incomes, so the Church was really getting a discount.

I wondered how much it cost in donated time and money to bring in each convert. Probably ten to twenty thousand dollars, I thought, even at minimum wage. Another ten thousand if you threw in the cost of bringing them back to church a second time. I'd actually done some calculations in the margin of my journal.

No wonder it was so important for Carl and me to keep them active.

I opened my eyes and looked over at Carl, so intent in his scriptures, and prayed to Heavenly Father for forgiveness again, for thinking about souls in such crass terms.

I wished I could crash a local quilting club and bear my testimony while the women sewed. Bring in a whole bevy of gifted crafters to the Relief Society. I wanted to visit a nursing home and save some souls just in the nick of time. I wanted to go to a Tupperware party and find some stay-at-home moms who still understood their place in the world.

I wanted to make the world a better place.

I looked at my watch and wondered if I should give Sister Penderly another call later in the week or just show up on her doorstep Sunday morning without giving her a chance to back out.

Carl was leaning back on the sofa now, his scriptures in his lap, his eyes closed. He looked so old when he was sleeping. He'd started snoring a couple of years ago.

I checked my laptop again. Still no messages. Kids these days didn't understand the importance of families.

Then I had an idea. I looked at Carl again and wondered if I could do it. Calling home was a big infraction, but I wanted to hear Valerie's and Susan's voices again. Even Jobeth's. I eased myself quietly off the sofa and went to the bedroom. I picked up the phone.

"Mom!" said Susan, surprised. "Are you okay?"

"Just thinking of you. I asked the president for permission to call."

"Oh." Why did she sound disappointed?

"So what's been going on with you guys? How's Phil?"

"Phil hates his job, just like always. But he can't get an interview anywhere else. It's all he talks about. And then he says he hates talking about it. But he never stops."

Wow, I thought. I sometimes forgot how good I had it with God as my boss. "And you?" I asked. "Are you doing anything fun? Treating yourself well?"

There was a long pause. "I'm seeing a therapist."

My mouth fell open. "Not the bishop? Whatever for?"

Susan laughed. "Did you not hear what I just said? Phil is making life miserable. I used to have you to talk to, but…"

I frowned. Was she trying to make me feel guilty for serving the Lord? That wasn't like her. She must really be feeling bad. "We have email, you know."

Silence on the other end.

"Well, things are going great here," I said. "We're reactivating a woman this week."

"Yes, I read your note."

This was not going the way I had hoped. She was supposed to be lifting my spirits. I was supposed to be lifting hers. That was the point of everything. "So how are Valerie and Steven?" I asked, hoping a change of subject might lighten things up. "How is Jobeth? Is Valerie expecting again?"

There was another long pause. Had my own daughter forgotten how to talk to me? I'd always faithfully emphasized the importance of the family unit. That families were forever. But she was being deliberately cool and distant. Had she lost the Spirit? I wasn't going to be around forever. At some point, she had to learn to start taking care of herself.

"Valerie and Steven have been having a rough time," Susan said slowly.

"Is he having trouble at work, too?" I sighed. "The economy is so bad. We should have elected Romney."

"They've asked to have their names removed from the membership rolls."

Now I was silent a long moment.

"You okay, Mom? I didn't want to tell you, but Valerie said she was going to write."

"But...but why?" I asked.

"They read about Church history on the internet."

"That's ridiculous!" I said. "You don't go to unproven sources for information. You go to the horse's mouth. Who knows more about Church history than the Church?"

Susan laughed humorlessly. "Apparently, almost everyone who pays attention. The first counselor in the stake presidency left last month. And I know two other families in our ward who are thinking of resigning. People are leaving in droves."

77

"What?" I asked. "Susan, this is my *job*. I would know if such a thing were happening. People are coming *back*. They're not leaving."

There was the sound of rustling on the other end of the phone, but I couldn't tell what it was. "I used to be angry at you for not being here to help us while we were struggling," said Susan, "but now I see it really wouldn't have made any difference."

"You're not leaving, too, are you?" I asked, aghast. What would happen to all our temple sealings?

"Phil stopped attending a few months ago. It's only a matter of time." There was a pause. "You may as well know. David has given up his callings. He still goes to church, but the writing is on the wall."

How could this be happening? David had just finished his own mission a few months ago. The Adversary must be focusing on my family because of the work I was doing. It frightened me, and I glanced about the room to see if there were any unexplained shadows flittering about. But such attention also proved just how important this work really was. I looked toward the living room and wondered if I should get Carl on the line. Perhaps I had been inspired by the Holy Ghost to make the call in the first place. Please, Heavenly Father, let me help my family.

Could I ask the mission president to contact the president of the mission back home and assign a missionary couple to them?

"Don't worry, Mom. We all love you. Everything is going to be okay."

They were all going to hell. How was that okay?

"Gotta go, Mom. I'll write you next week."

The phone went dead. I stood staring at it for the longest time. Wasn't Heavenly Father supposed to bestow extra blessings on our family because of our service? I didn't understand. What was going on?

Thank goodness Richard was dead.

I walked back out to the living room in a daze and sat down gently on the sofa. I pulled the scriptures carefully out of his hands and opened to a page at random. I looked at Carl. He was dedicated. I was dedicated. He and I were going to the Celestial Kingdom, and we'd have more children there. We'd people an entire planet with righteous children.

Family still mattered.

I searched the page in front of me for inspiration, something I could tell Sister Penderly to make sure she came back.

But my eyes wouldn't focus and I couldn't make out the words.

I held the book against my chest, feeling the pounding of my heart, and listened to Carl snoring quietly beside me.

Born on the Sixth of April

My companion kept looking down at his hands and twitching his fingers. "You okay?" I whispered.

"Candy Crush would make this conference a lot more bearable," Elder Collins whispered back. "It's how I used to get through Sacrament meeting."

An elder behind us cleared his throat, and we went back to listening to the testimonies at zone conference. We'd made it through President Banner's talk chastising us for not baptizing more converts here in Des Moines. And of course there were other reproachful talks by both of the Assistants to the President, who seemed to feel they were on the fast track to apostleship. They explained that unless we were teaching a golden family every evening, we were proving that we didn't have enough faith. Some of the other missionaries actually enjoyed conference, as it was an all-day affair that guaranteed the absence of proselytizing, but to me, it was just a waste of time. The others seemed to accept living in an eternal state of guilt, while I refused to succumb to it. I would rather have been on the street with my companion doing something useful.

It was just like my time in Phoenix, I thought. Missions were the same everywhere.

The sister currently bearing her testimony finished, and another missionary took her place behind the microphone. "I'd like to thank Heavenly Father for sending me to Iowa," he began, "and for giving me such an awesome companion. We both get so psyched preaching the gospel and building up Zion here."

These guys were in my district, though in a different apartment. Everyone knew they simply made up their stats every week. President Banner must surely know it, too. But he looked on with a contented smile as the testimony bubbled on.

It was a mistake in my opinion to treat the mission like a business. We had devotionals every morning and district meetings every week which were essentially sales meetings. Our letters to the president were status reports not on our spiritual well-being but on our business goals. How many lessons did we teach? How many times did we ask the Golden Questions? How many investigators did we get to church? How many baptisms did we have? It was like attending a board meeting and going over the company's financials. And just as important as the figures themselves was our effort at displaying the "right attitude." No matter how poorly someone had performed at what was essentially an impossible task, you had to promise you'd really do it next time. You knew you were lying. They knew you were lying. But there was always the hope that somehow if you felt guilty enough, you could make God perform the miracle for you.

Not that anyone cared what I thought about all of this. But they would one day, I thought. One day.

Another elder stood up and began speaking. "I know this church is the only true church on the face of the Earth. I know President Monson is a prophet of God. I know the Book of Mormon is true."

Interesting, I thought. Why wasn't he adding, "I know my father will buy me a car if I last the whole two years out here"?

Everyone knew that was why he was pretending to be a missionary. President Banner knew as well.

I looked over at Elder Collins. His fingers were twitching. I caught his eye and smiled. He rolled his in return. He was here for a better reason than that of the elder bearing his testimony. Elder Collins had been promised four years of tuition by his father if he served his time.

It was difficult to see so many unhappy people out here. The sisters usually seemed a little more content, since they didn't have to serve unless they wanted to. But many of the guys needed Prozac to get through the day. Leadership seemed to be all about guilt as motivation, and that led inevitably to misery. One of my companions had a couple of porn magazines hidden in his suitcase. Another actually chewed Nicorette whenever he found the chance. Missionaries were always at the mercy of their companions. Would the infractions be reported or would their companion look the other way?

I always looked the other way. It wasn't that I didn't think the infractions were a problem. I simply tried to see the bigger picture. It wasn't a talent that many of our Church leaders had, and it was why I was out here serving a second mission in the first place.

Every single one of my companions had let their mouths drop open in horror when they discovered this was my second time around. "But *why?*" they'd ask, their brows furrowed in confusion, using the same tone they'd employ if they were asking a man why he'd had a testicle deliberately removed.

"I was born on the sixth of April," I would reply with a smile. Christ's birthday. I couldn't very well explain my real reasons. I had graduated from college at eighteen and served my first mission at the usual age. Then I'd gone home and earned my PhD in Psychology within three more years and decided to serve a second time while I was still young enough to pass for twenty.

"My companion and I had the most incredible experience this week," a sister missionary was now saying at the front of the room. "A man sicced his huge dog after us, and we ran as fast as we could, but the dog was gaining on us. Then Sister Campos turned around and said, 'In the name of Jesus Christ, we command you to stop,' and the dog just stopped, looked at us a minute, and calmly walked away. Heavenly Father truly protects his servants."

Elder Collins turned to look at me and shrugged, impressed by the story.

Our spiritual fuel was a series of anecdotes, half of which were exaggerated, most of the others being downright fabrications. Did no one remember Paul H. Dunn?

It didn't have to be this way.

Studying psychology for all those years taught me a great deal about the human mind. I decided that the world was too big a place to make a difference on a global scale, but if I concentrated on the small environment of Mormonism, I might be able to create some tiny change. I knew the Church usually chose successful businessmen and attorneys to be General Authorities, but I planned to make such a splash in the world that they'd have to at least consider me. And I'd persuade them that they *needed* someone with my talents in the Quorum of the Twelve to deal with modern society. Only someone who truly understood how the mind worked would be able to guide members successfully through life. For decades, the leaders had felt that Correlation was the answer to controlling everyone's thoughts. They still didn't realize that in today's world, there was no longer any possibility of control. Or that control was a bad idea to begin with. They needed a new approach but simply didn't have the skills to develop one. I knew I could guide the members down the right path by illuminating that path more clearly.

First, though, I needed to guide the other leaders, who were most definitely going down the wrong path themselves.

It wasn't apostasy to admit that the leaders were wrong. They were dealing with an outdated model of behavior. Anyone who knew the least bit about applied behavior analysis or project-based learning could see it plainly.

"I'd like to thank Heavenly Father for the opportunity to be here," another elder began. "And for our great mission president, and for my companion and my zone leaders. I'd even like to thank Heavenly Father for the lack of success we've had in the work lately. It's kept me humble, and I know the Lord can't do anything through me unless I'm humble. So even when things don't look like they're going well, I know the Lord is still behind it all. It's comforting to be able to recognize his hand at every step in my life."

I closed my eyes in disgust but opened them when Elder Collins nudged me in the ribs. He was grinning. Even he knew what the elder was saying was complete rubbish.

If we knew it, surely the president knew it, too. I thought about Pinker's work on innuendo and euphemism. The elephant in the living room.

I hated zone conference. Even with all my years of training, it was hard to withstand such a heavy onslaught of warped thinking. How did the leaders do it? Improving the mental culture of the Church would help *everyone*. I simply had to rise through the ranks so I would eventually have the power to do something.

Only half of the missionaries had borne their testimonies so far, and I knew the president would wait until every last one of us had gotten up in front of the others. It was part of the continual effort at control. I stole a glance at my watch. Then I realized the president had been looking right at me at that very moment. Oops.

I paid more attention to the next few testimonies. One elder spoke about how he called an anti-Mormon to repentance the week before. Another cried as he told us how the Lord touched his heart every day when he read the scriptures. A sister explained how she knew this experience would make her a better wife later. Elder Collins nudged me in the ribs again and made a face. Sister Blumquist wasn't very pretty.

I found myself growing more and more annoyed as the meeting dragged on. Every single missionary had to hit the four high points in their testimony. 1.) The Church was true. 2.) The Book of Mormon was true. 3.) Joseph Smith was a prophet of God. 4.) President Monson was a prophet of God. No matter what else was said, these points absolutely had to be made. And everyone knew it. And everyone was merely checking them off a list. But forcing people to swear loyalty publicly didn't actually create loyalty. It mostly created liars. I knew for a fact that several of these guys didn't believe a single word of what they were saying. Half the missionaries were speaking out of guilt, and the other half out of pressure.

Science told me there was a better way.

Finally, the remaining missionaries who hadn't yet stood up were getting fewer and farther between. Elder Collins walked to the microphone and said, "I'm grateful for the opportunity to serve a mission. I'm grateful for my companion, who makes the work such fun. I'm grateful..." I could see the president staring at me carefully as my companion continued. Fun wasn't a good word. This was serious business. I stared back at him calmly. I was still just a senior companion after all this time. I'd thought surely on my second go around I'd rise up faster in the mission hierarchy. I needed to have leadership experience if I wanted to become a bishop before I was thirty, a stake president before I was thirty-five. But for some reason President Banner clearly didn't like me.

I'd have to change that. I'd have to say something absolutely remarkable when I bore my testimony.

Maybe I'd tell the truth.

I waited for another elder and another sister, and then I walked up to the podium. "Elders and Sisters," I began bluntly, "the Church has got it all wrong." I paused, hearing several loud gasps from the audience. "We spend so much of our time trying to prove we're Christians, that we're just like everyone else, that we're not scary, that people should relax around us. But that's the wrong approach. I'm not here to teach sinners. I'm here to teach future gods. And I let my investigators know that up front. We're different from other religions, and that's a good thing. In fact, it's the most important thing we have to offer, the only reason anyone should pay attention to us in the first place."

I heard some throat-clearing behind me on the stand, some shifting in the seats.

"It's why I've baptized ten people so far, way more than the mission average. You don't tell people all the things they're doing wrong and make them feel like dirt that needs to be washed away. You convince them they're gods in embryo. That's what we're here to do." I went on for a couple more minutes explaining some of the things I'd learned in school and why they should try the course of action I proposed if they wanted to see real success.

I deliberately did not mention a single one of the four required parts of a testimony. I closed in the name of Jesus Christ and walked back to my seat. All eyes were on me.

We talked about the Celestial Kingdom amongst ourselves all the time and knew exactly what that meant. But in public we pretended we didn't all want to be gods. It was the driving force behind everything we did, and yet we hid that fact from every prospective convert. How did we ever expect them to be interested in what interested us, when we were teaching them something different than we were teaching ourselves?

The Church had it wrong. We should be shouting this from the rooftops. Talking about our future planets. Our future galaxies. Not hiding what we really believed. We were *supposed* to be a "peculiar" people.

I'd been wrong, too. I'd been trying to move up the chain of command in the traditional way, but after today, I would be called as a zone leader for sure. Leaders recognized other leaders. That was Heifetz's leadership psychology.

The rest of the meeting was rather subdued, but before long, every last missionary had borne his or her testimony. Finally, one of the elders was called to give a closing prayer, and we were through for the day. It was almost 5:00. "There's still time to teach a couple of lessons before the evening is done," the president reminded us with a smile as we stood to leave. Then he pointed at me and motioned for me to come over.

Two days later, I was on a flight back home. I hadn't even been allowed to say good-bye to any of our investigators. I sat on the plane with my scriptures packed away, my head still spinning. Other missionaries would try to talk to their seatmates, I thought. But I knew the way people thought. No one wanted to be trapped next to someone like that.

The leaders just didn't understand the way the mind worked. The Church had everything wrong.

I looked out the window and wondered what the stigma would be like for serving thirty-eight months instead of a mere twenty-four. What bishop would call someone who'd been sent home to be Elders Quorum president or first counselor in the bishopric?

What respectable Mormon girl would ever date me?

I thought about the work of Les Parrott and Alice Miller. All my years of education, and I was never going to be able to make life better for anyone.

I looked down at my hands and suddenly felt very, very guilty.

Missionaries by Moonlight

"Toothpaste."

"El dentifríco."

"Shower."

"La ducha."

"To put clothes on. To dress oneself."

"Vestirse."

My companion closed his book. "Elder Romano, don't you think we can learn something a little more relevant?"

"You've got to start somewhere, Elder Petrakis," I replied. "We need to be able to say everyday things first."

"I suppose. But it's so frustrating not even being able to conjugate yet."

"Keep going."

He sighed. "Tie."

"La corbata."

"To eat."

"Comer."

Elder Petrakis and I had been together in northeast Atlanta for only two weeks before we made a startling discovery—

while both of us still believed the Mormon Church was true, neither of us wanted to be out here for two years serving as missionaries. That's when we made our pact, to spend most of our time studying so we'd be better prepared when we were finally allowed to attend college, and exercising heavily to stay in shape. We simply made up the stats every week which we reported to our leaders. It had worked out for the past seven weeks so far, and since we'd just had transfers a week ago, it appeared we'd be together for at least three more weeks before the next set was issued.

It was going to be difficult going back to regular missionary work after we'd tasted freedom, so we planned to make the most of it while we could. Elder Petrakis still had over a year left, and I had six more months. It was unheard of for missionaries to be kept together for more than three or four months. We had to make up stories to tell the other missionaries, as well as our families and girlfriends back home, but we used the time in Companion Inventory to correlate what we'd say.

We kept up our Spanish lesson this morning until 9:00. Then we closed our books.

"Already?" asked Elder Petrakis.

"I know, but we've got to get dressed. The zone leaders can pop in any time after 9:30 to make sure we're out of the apartment like we're supposed to be."

"It'd be a lot easier if we could stay in."

"The president would have an emergency transfer if he found what we were up to."

Elder Petrakis nodded. "Twelve hours outside the apartment is a lot of time to kill."

"We'll walk for a couple of hours before it gets too hot. Then we'll go to the library to read more of that English history textbook we found." We'd searched the shelves until we found two identical copies of a book and read the same chapters together. "Quiz each other on what we learned. And then head to the gym."

"How long before a member discovers us somewhere not working?"

I shrugged. "What choice do we have? You want to go back to tracting door to door?"

He stuck out his tongue. "So what's our community service going to be this afternoon, Elder Romano?"

While we could only count four hours of service a week on our stats without being reprimanded, my companion and I typically did four hours every single day. You could only study and lift weights just so many hours, after all. And we did want to feel we were doing something useful while we were out here. We simply weren't interested in preaching. Everyone had different talents, but all young Mormon men were forced to do the same thing. It didn't mean the Church wasn't true. Only that it wasn't as efficient as it thought it was. And could be.

"How about we man the AA hotline again?" I suggested. Yesterday, we'd manned the suicide hotline.

Elder Petrakis nodded. "Sounds good." I was lucky to have such an agreeable companion. Most complained about even the easiest types of work. There were only so many kinds of service we could do while sporting white shirts and ties, and we couldn't go out in jeans for fear the ZLs would be waiting for us when we returned home. This must be what undocumented immigrants felt like all the time, I thought, constantly in fear of being discovered. Or gays who were still in the closet. Or atheists at Brigham Young University.

Elder Petrakis and I did our morning "chores" and then headed to the gym shortly after noon. We ran through all the regular exercises as usual. While I was spotting Elder Petrakis, another young man with a washboard stomach came up to us. It was wonderful to be here in just our gym shorts, our flesh exposed to the air. I felt free in a way that I never did when bearing my testimony. And we weren't even Mormon women, never allowed to so much as reveal a shoulder. Guys were lucky. Even Mormon guys. "How long you two been together?" asked the young man.

My heart skipped a beat. He could tell we were companions. Was he a member? "About two months," I said, trying to sound casual.

"Really? You guys look like you've been married for ages. You get along so well."

Elder Petrakis almost dropped the barbell. "We're not gay!" he said.

The young man frowned, so I clarified. "We don't have any problem with gays. But Donovan and I are just friends."

Elder Petrakis gave me a look, but I'd told the truth. My companion and I had talked at length about issues we had with Church doctrine and policies. The treatment of gays and lesbians was just one of them. And its views on the "role" of women. It was what made proselytizing so difficult. The Church may have been true, but that didn't mean it wasn't wrong.

"I'm Steve," said the young man, offering his hand. I shook it, and then Elder Petrakis sat up and shook Steve's hand hesitantly as well.

The young man looked us up and down, and I thought he was going to proposition us despite what I'd just said. "What do you guys do for a living?" he asked.

Elder Petrakis and I stole a glance. "We're students," I replied. "On scholarship." The truth was that my companion's father was paying for his mission entirely. I'd only managed to save up about half of the funds necessary for my own, so my father was helping me out as well. We both felt guilty for using the funds dishonestly. But our families would have been a lot unhappier if we'd simply gone home before our time was up.

And life wouldn't have been so great for us, either. We'd both face not getting help with tuition, and we'd be treated like apostates, even though we both still believed. It must be how a homeless person felt, ignored by everyone who walked by.

"Do you guys need to make a little extra cash?" Steve persisted.

I couldn't tell where this line of questioning was leading, but I was beginning to feel more uncomfortable. Was he going to ask us to help him sell steroids? I wasn't sure I wanted to bother disapproving, but it certainly wasn't something I wanted to do.

"Yes, we could use a little money," said Elder Petrakis.

I turned to him.

"My scholarship may not be renewed."

Steve smiled. "I work at this place called Peter's Pole." Elder Petrakis and I looked at each other. "I'm a dancer. And two of our dancers just moved to New York, so we could really use some help. You guys would be perfect."

"But...but we're not gay," Elder Petrakis repeated.

Steve laughed. "Most of the dancers aren't."

"I don't understand," I said.

Some other guys wanted to use the bench and the weights, so Steve motioned for us to follow him. We grabbed our towels and headed to the locker room. "It's easy," he said. "You get some music and dance for five minutes. We go in rotations, so your turn might come up once an hour or so."

"How much do we make?" asked Elder Petrakis.

"Depends. The bar only gives you a base rate. You make most of the rest in tips."

"Tips?" I asked.

"The men aren't allowed to touch you, so they'll throw dollars on the stage. You put them in your G-string."

I was beginning to feel uncomfortable again.

"We can do that, can't we, El—I mean, can't we, Garrett?" My companion looked happier than I'd seen him since I suggested eating doughnuts on Fast Sunday.

"And of course, there's always the possibility of dates," Steve went on.

"Dates?" I asked.

"It all has to be unofficial, naturally, but some of the men will meet you in the lounge and arrange for a private date. You can charge two or three hundred for things like that."

"We won't be going on any dates," I said.

"Suit yourself. The dancing itself is fun, though. And even just with that, you can make some good money. You guys want to come to the club tonight and see what it's like?"

He gave us the address and then headed for the showers. Elder Petrakis and I sat down on a bench fingering our towels for a long time. Another man noisily banged the door of his locker and looked at us with disdain. I had no idea what he thought we were doing.

"We'll be sent home," I said after the man left.

"I want to do it."

"Why?" I couldn't hide my surprise.

Elder Petrakis shrugged. "I want to do something amazing with my life. Not be ordinary."

"Pole dancing is what people at the bottom of the barrel do, not those who are achieving greatness."

"Sheesh, you sound just like a Mormon."

I had to laugh at that. "Perhaps you're right," I said, wiping my face with my towel. If I couldn't see the Eiffel Tower or ride in a gondola on the Grand Canal, my options for adventure were limited. "We'll go after 10:30. The ZLs will never check on us after lights out. It can't hurt just to look."

Elder Petrakis nodded with a smile and then echoed my thoughts. "If the Church won't send us somewhere interesting overseas, we'll just have to make do with what we've got." We really were a good fit, I realized. Heavenly Father must have arranged for us to be assigned together. God could be a nice guy sometimes.

Though I still wished I could have gone to Japan.

In the afternoon, we took a few calls from people desperate not to take a drink, and we guided them to various meetings. Perhaps we weren't making much of a difference in the world, but it was better than having doors shut in our faces. The truth was, whatever stats we turned in to our leaders, our actual numbers weren't all that different from what other missionaries who were working full-time were getting. So many people these days didn't care about religion, and the ones who did didn't care about Mormonism. Sooner or later, the Church was going to have to figure out a different approach.

But that wasn't my problem. My task was not to be sent home early in disgrace. Go to college, marry Charlotte in the temple, and hang in there until the Church became a place I actually wanted to bring my friends to.

Sometimes, I wondered if I was wasting my time.

I cooked fish patties and tater tots for dinner, Elder Petrakis and I visited a couple of inactive families, and then we went back to the apartment to change into our P-day clothes. "I'm a little nervous," I said. It must be how a woman at BYU felt deciding to study business. Or physics.

"It's not like the mission president will be there," Elder Petrakis pointed out.

We drove carefully to the club, which was outside our zone, and I worried about the mileage we had to keep track of. We'd just have to conserve over the next few days. The building looked unspectacular from the outside, but there were a good many cars in the parking lot, even though it was a Thursday night. Elder Petrakis was smiling as we climbed out of the car.

Two Mormon missionaries going to a gay strip club. I could see the look on my parents' faces if they ever found out.

Inside, we paid a cover, which meant skipping a meal tomorrow. Several men gave us piercing stares, but we ignored them and sat a few seats away from the runway. Elder Petrakis was still smiling. For someone who didn't want to be thought of as gay, he was fitting in awfully well. We watched in the darkened room as dancer after dancer strutted out on stage. The men in the audience were surprisingly quiet, staring in rapt attention, but rarely smiling even when they liked someone enough to put money on the platform.

But it wasn't as if anyone was masturbating in the audience. No one on stage was showing their penis. It all seemed innocent enough.

I laughed at myself.

When Steve came out on stage, I went up and put two dollar bills by his foot. He looked down at me and smiled. After he finished, he walked out into the crowd to meet us. Everyone was staring at him in admiration. "Follow me," he said. We walked down a hall into a lounge area.

"You came! I'm so glad. Let me introduce you to the manager."

I was about to protest that we hadn't made up our minds yet, but the smile on my companion's face told me we had. What had started out weeks ago as a desire to learn a second language had somehow spiraled completely out of control.

This was what happened to people who broke the commandments.

We spoke with the manager, took off our T-shirts to show what we could offer, and agreed to come to the club two nights a week to begin with, Thursdays and Sundays. We'd start in just a few days. I had to admit, the idea of being a sex object was exciting, even if it wasn't anything I could ever tell my girlfriend waiting patiently at home for me.

Steve appeared to receive some kind of finder's fee for recruiting us, but he seemed genuinely happy for us as well. He hurried off to mingle with some older men, and I shrugged. "Seen enough for one night?" I asked Elder Petrakis. "We'd better get home so we don't oversleep in the morning." I shook my head. "We sure don't want to be caught in bed if the ZLs make a surprise visit."

I felt a tap on my shoulder. "Elder Romano?" a voice asked.

I shivered and felt my stomach drop. I turned and looked into the face of Bishop Sanders, the bishop of the last ward where I'd served. "Uh, hi there," I said. Elder Petrakis was looking on with wide eyes. His smile was gone.

"Looks like you guys are doing some moonlighting." He smiled, and there was no malice in his face. It dawned on me that no one who was going to see me here was in a position to complain about it.

"Well, Bish—" I began.

"It's Clark here," he interrupted.

"Clark," I agreed.

"We're not gay," said Elder Petrakis.

Bishop Sanders laughed. I suddenly remembered that he had a wife and five children at home. I felt bad for all seven of them. He saw my look and shrugged, but his smile faded. "Reality isn't always pretty."

I thought about alcoholics going to meetings, and desperate people fighting not to commit suicide, and Latinos trying to get day labor at Home Depot.

And missionaries fudging stats.

"You're right about that," I said. Elder Petrakis looked like he was calming down a little. "Just so you know, our nights here are Thursdays and Sundays. Though I can't imagine you manage to get away from home very often."

He shook his head sadly. In fact, he looked so forlorn that it made me try to think of more ideas for community service.

"We're not going to do dates for just anybody," I said, watching my companion's eyes grow larger as I spoke. "But we'll do it for members."

"Saving up for college?" asked Bishop Sanders with a tiny smile. "I take it you're not going to BYU."

"We'll donate all the money to Amnesty International," I said, and this time it was the bishop who looked surprised. There were other older men in the room nearby talking to other young men, making deals of their own.

"Are you guys really straight?" he asked.

We looked at each other and nodded.

"Then why are you doing this?"

I held out my upturned hands in front of me. "We're all trying to get through life as best we can," I said, thinking of all the months I had left before I could return home. "And in the meantime we're here to serve."

"No tithing on your secondary income?" he asked with a smile.

"Two years of our life is tithing enough."

The bishop nodded. We all stood there in awkward silence another few moments, and then Bishop Sanders spoke. "I'd say my place or yours, but we know what the answer to that has to be." He paused and then motioned toward the door. "Shall we?" He started off down the hall, and we followed.

"Elder Romano," Elder Petrakis whispered. "What are we going to do?"

I turned to him and whispered back. "Whatever he wants us to." I clapped my hand on his shoulder. "You wanted something amazing, and now you're going to get it."

"¡Ay, caramba!"

We drove home, with the bishop close on our tail. He got even closer on our tails once he was inside the apartment, and Elder Petrakis and I both lost our virginity that night. I found myself rather unfazed by the entire experience, as if this were all the most natural thing in the world.

Did the Church try to scare us from everyday things just to keep us in line? Even gay sex for a straight man seemed surprisingly ordinary. But it definitely crossed a line.

What was the point of that line?

I was going to have to tell Charlotte about all this one day. I hoped she'd still want to get married in the temple.

"I'll put in a word with the mission president," the bishop said. "See if I can't keep you two together as long as possible."

"Thanks, Bishop," I said.

"Clark."

"Thanks, Clark."

"I'm sore," said Elder Petrakis.

The bishop laughed and gave us each a hug before heading out the door. I took the two hundred dollars he'd left us and put it in a sock. Every penny of it would go to charity. If we had to skip another meal to pay for the dancing attire, so be it. I tucked the sock away and then motioned for Elder Petrakis to kneel with me beside our beds. We bowed our heads and had companion prayer before sliding back under the sheets.

And for the first time since I'd been set apart all those months ago by my stake president back home with my parents watching proudly, I finally felt good to be a missionary.

Starting a Leper Colony

"How have things been going for you lately, Burt?" asked Bishop Wilson, his hands clasped in a serene fashion on top of his desk. He smiled at me kindly. "You seem a little down." I was having a routine interview with the bishop of my ward in east Dallas. We talked every six months.

"Oh, I'm okay," I replied. "It's just…"

"What?"

I looked at the bishop. He was the one person in the ward who knew my secret, so these talks twice a year were the only chance I had to open up to anyone. And yet…

Bishop Wilson looked at his watch and then showed his smile again. "What is it, Burt?" He nodded at me encouragingly.

"I'll be turning fifty next month."

"Yes. Yes. Congratulations."

"What I mean is, my life feels almost over, and I've never even started to live it yet."

The bishop shook his head and pointed to a painting of the Second Coming on the wall of his office. "You've almost made it, Burt. You just need to remain faithful a little longer. Once you're on the other side, everything will be wonderful. You'll see."

"But the Church teaches that we're the same people after we die. My personality isn't going to change the instant my spirit leaves my body. Won't I still be me?"

"Well, of course you will."

"So I'll be gay in the Spirit World, too."

Bishop Wilson looked at his watch again. "The Lord will take care of everything. You just need to have faith." He smiled again, a little less vibrantly.

"If I didn't have faith," I replied curtly, "I wouldn't still be a virgin at forty-nine, would I?"

The bishop peered at me a long moment as if not sure of the answer. Two of my previous bishops over the years had told me if I had "legitimate" faith, I could change. The very first bishop I had come out to, shortly after my mission, had wanted to ask the stake president to start proceedings against me. Only after I convinced him I was absolutely committed to celibacy had he relented. Attitudes had grown a little kinder over the years, but each bishop always looked like he'd rather be talking about almost anything else. Bishop Wilson made a sincere effort, and I appreciated it, but even he believed my "condition" deep down was all my own fault. After another moment of scrutiny, he finally pointed vaguely toward me and said, "How's that red patch on your face doing?"

I instinctively touched the area near my nose. I'd had rosacea for decades. Desonide lotion helped, but my face never cleared up completely. As a pharmacist, I saw all the other treatments out there, too. Nothing worked perfectly. I was about to answer the bishop when I suddenly realized the implication of the question. "You think it hasn't been hard for me to stay a virgin because I'm not the handsomest guy in the world?" I asked. "I haven't masturbated in years. I could do that no matter how ugly I am."

"I didn't mean any such thing," said the bishop soothingly. "I was just asking after your health."

I rubbed my knees and looked at the floor a long moment. Then I turned back to the bishop. "The Three Nephites asked for a special blessing," I said, "to live forever. Would it be a sin for me to ask for a special blessing, too? To die soon?"

"Now, now, Burt. It isn't as bad as all that. You just need to listen to more CDs from the Mormon Tabernacle Choir. Read the scriptures more. You'll be fine. The commandment is to endure to the end." He smiled, the vibrant one again. "You're doing a great job teaching the Elders Quorum. Keep up the good work." He stood and offered his hand.

I shook it, forcing a smile of my own. Bishop Wilson wasn't a bad man, I realized. He was an accountant with a wife and three kids, overworked and completely untrained for pastoral care. Having a lay leadership was supposed to be one of the signs that we were the true church. But it also meant I'd had to travel this road mostly alone for the past thirty years.

I drove home, put on a CD, and sipped my favorite sparkling mineral water. Only I wasn't listening to Motab. I was listening to the music I liked best, a compilation of my favorite 1980's music. Debbie Gibson, Air Supply, REO Speedwagon, Men at Work, and others. I loved George Michael, the Bangles, Belinda Carlisle, and Heart. I absolutely adored Roxette. I even listened to some Madonna, as decadent as she might be. She still had some good songs.

The 1980's had been so great.

I'd graduated high school here in Dallas during that wonderful decade. I'd gone on a mission to Colombia. I'd finished college in Austin. The 1980's was my coming of age, and the songs that recorded those moments in my brain would always be important to me.

If you could say that someone who had never been on a single date in his whole life had actually ever come of age. In some ways, I was still fourteen.

And it wasn't only my taste in music that had stopped in time. It was almost as if my whole personality had done so as well. I had never bought a cell phone. I rarely used the computer, and when I did, it was to check the occasional email I received. I didn't tweet or blog or download those songs I loved so much. I didn't pay my bills electronically. I didn't shop online. While I was technically on Facebook, forced by a family member, I probably only logged in once a month. There was never anything new there to bother with.

What was the point of living a modern life, if the only time I had ever been truly happy was a brief period of three months in Bogotá when I was twenty?

I went to my office and studied my computer. The machine was eleven years old, ancient in computer years. I'd have to buy a new one soon. I logged on and checked my email. There was an advertisement from Deseret Book for a new LDS movie. A notice that my library book was due back in two days. A fundraising request from the Leprosy Foundation, one of the few charities I donated to regularly.

I thought about checking Facebook, but the idea exhausted me.

Maybe the White Pages, I thought. The internet had to be good for something. On a whim, I looked up the name of my favorite missionary companion. With a last name like McKessins, he might not be too hard to find. Of course, you had to enter a city, and since I hadn't spoken to him in three decades, that was a little problematic.

I remembered he was from St. George, so I tried that first, but there was nothing. Maybe Salt Lake, I thought, but he wasn't there, either. Las Vegas wasn't far from St. George. Perhaps he'd ended up in that city. But no. I bit my lip, staring at the screen, knowing I couldn't very well look up every city in the country.

What was the point of having a computer if it didn't tell you what you needed to know? I prayed for revelation.

Well, Elder McKessins had sometimes talked about wanting to see San Francisco, I mused, so I supposed that was worth a shot. I typed in his name, clicked enter, and sure enough there was one hit.

Oh, my Lord. Was it that easy? Could I have done this years ago? He was such a great guy back in the day. Surely, he still was. Could I have really had a friend all this time? I looked at my phone and reached for the receiver. Then I stopped myself. The man was Mormon. I knew what that meant. His whole life revolved around his current ward and callings. He'd be polite, even friendly. We'd have a nice twenty minute conversation, he'd tell me about his work and his kids, and I'd never hear from him again. It almost sounded worse than not talking at all.

"Heavenly Father," I prayed, "I've been as faithful as the Three Nephites. Can't you grant my wish, too? Can't you take me now?"

I looked up at the ceiling as if expecting...something...and then looked at my phone again. The lyrics to Go West's "King of Wishful Thinking" ran through my mind. I picked up the receiver and dialed.

The guy on the other end, even if it was him, would probably screen his calls and ignore the unfamiliar number on his Caller ID. I was probably calling another land line to begin with. People didn't answer land lines. People only answered cell phones these days. I knew that much about technology.

After four rings, I got cold feet and started to replace the receiver. Then I heard someone pick up. My heart beat faster.

"Hello?"

"May...may I speak with Gerald McKessins?" I asked.

"What can I do for you?"

I tried to use my best Colombian accent as I said in Spanish, "It's your old junior companion, Elder Jackson."

There was silence on the other end of the phone for a long moment, and I began to think I'd called the wrong Gerald McKessins. I was just about to say something when the man said, in English, "Oh, my god."

Hmm. That didn't sound like a Mormon thing to say. "How have you been?" I asked.

"Fine. Fine. I'm a dermatologist, practicing here in San Francisco. Have a great home with a wonderful view. Still in good shape, run every day. Watch the telenovelas once in a while to keep up my Spanish." He laughed, and then there was silence.

That was it, I thought? That was his summary of three decades? We'd been so close all those years ago. I felt a little disappointed, but to be fair, just how close could two people be who'd only known each other a few weeks? In the back of my mind, I'd always fantasized about attending a mission reunion and running into him. Had thought about visiting him and becoming friends again, keeping in touch. I had wanted to feel close to someone again. Three months out of an entire lifetime wasn't very much. And it didn't look like I was going to get so much as a single day more.

"And you?" he asked. "What have you done with your life?"

Now I was the one to pause, wanting to hang up rather than answer that question honestly. "Nothing at all," I finally said.

Another long silence. This was hopeless, a waste of time. I now felt worse than I had to begin with.

"Elder Jackson…"

"Burt," I corrected.

"Burt, you're not married?"

I laughed. "Gerald, I'm still a virgin."

"What?"

I needed to have at least one other person besides the bishop know who I was. "I'm gay," I said.

"Oh, my god." There was another moment of silence, and my heart sank. It was stupid to think I could rekindle a friendship from thirty years ago, a relationship that had lasted a mere fraction of my lifetime. Maybe—

"I'm gay, too," Gerald said. "How did you know to call?"

And now I was silent again, too stupefied to answer, too much of a Luddite even to know how to use the old-fashioned telephone in my hand anymore. "I...I just missed you," I said. "I've never really had another friend since you were transferred away."

Sounding pathetic was hardly the way to win somebody over, I thought, but suddenly, the floodgates opened. We spent the next forty minutes catching up on all the details of life since our time together. He had more to tell than I did, of course. He'd come out and left the Church two years after his mission. He'd had three long-term relationships, none lasting more than a few years, and confessed to many casual ones in between. He'd gone to medical school, traveled the world, and appeared in a documentary about leprosy in Colombia. He did volunteer work there two weeks out of every year.

"I remember us talking about going back to Colombia after our missions," I said. "Starting a leper colony. Or teaching poor children. Or doing something to make a difference."

"But you still go to church," said Gerald. "Didn't you feel you were making a difference by spreading the gospel?"

"I suppose," I said slowly. "But I remember when we met that unfortunate man with the skin condition."

"Jesus," said Gerald.

"That's right. I guess I felt that he needed help I couldn't give. And that I should have been able to. It's why I became a pharmacist."

"He's one of the reasons I studied dermatology."

We talked another twenty minutes after that, and I felt something strange in my chest. I felt…like a glass that had just been filled with fresh water. And yet I felt something else at the same time, a void deeper than any I had ever experienced before.

I suddenly realized that talking to Gerald three times a year on the phone, or emailing him once a month, or checking his Facebook page once a week, wasn't going to cut it for me. Even seeing him in person on a once in a lifetime visit to the West Coast, or as much as once every year, wasn't going to help. I remembered crying the night after he'd been transferred to another city on the far side of the mission.

Maybe I'd better ask the bishop for another interview.

Finally, despite how little experience I had with long conversations, I could tell this one was drawing to an end. My heart started beating faster again. This might be it. We might never speak after this. I had to say it while I still had the chance, something I wished I had said thirty years ago.

"I've always loved you."

There was another silence, and I realized I'd broken the spell. I'd ruined our reunion. It was just like me to do such a thing. I was alone for a reason. Even single virgins had friends if they weren't totally clueless dweebs.

"Burt, I have to tell you some things before you go down that line of thinking." He paused and then said, "I have HIV, and I have genital warts." He laughed a little bitterly. "Two gifts from my last partner who used to cheat on me and then beat me for not being good enough to keep him faithful."

This was what life was like outside Mormonism.

Well, so be it.

"I'm a leper in the gay world," he continued. "But then, you're a gay Mormon. You know what it's like to be a leper among your own people."

"No one at church knows I'm gay," I said.

"And don't you still feel like you're covering your lesions every single day so no one sees the truth?"

I thought about Sacrament meeting, and Priesthood, and Gospel Doctrine, and Home Teaching. "I've never been to San Francisco," I said. "If I come for a visit, will you show me a good time?"

Another one of those infernal pauses. "Are you sure you know what you're getting yourself in for?"

"What do you call two lepers living together?" I asked in return.

"I don't know."

I laughed this time. "I don't know, either. But I'm willing to find out the answer."

"Find a flight, Burt. And we'll see what happens."

After we hung up, I sat in front of my computer, looking at my screen saver, a photo of a waterfall in Colombia. I clicked on Firefox, put Youtube in the address bar, and tried to remember a song I'd heard years before. I'd hated it at the time. It had seemed so wicked. I fiddled around with some possible titles and finally found the song I wanted by Dead or Alive. I hit play. The lyrics to "Brand New Lover" flowed out of my speakers.

I pulled my old mission album off the shelf and opened to the section with Elder McKessins. I looked at his picture, caressed his face, and thought about unzipping my pants. Then I decided to wait. It would make our first night together all the more memorable. Instead, I logged onto Facebook and updated my status. It was a bit premature, and I might have to change it back all too soon, but those words looked awfully nice.

In a relationship.

I didn't even know what he looked like these days. But I also knew I didn't care in the slightest. It remained to be seen, of course, if he felt the same way.

I Googled flights to San Francisco, found a travel site, and set up a user name and password. Then I made my first online purchase, a ticket to California in two weeks. I'd manage to schedule some leave from the pharmacy somehow. I had over eight weeks saved up.

I stripped to my garments and looked down at myself. Tomorrow after work, I'd have to go shopping for something more appropriate. I fingered the symbol sewn over the right breast. Strange how one could feel both sad and happy at the same time. I thought back to a television commercial I'd seen recently touting some new drug which I'd seen at work. It helped with a chronic health issue but came with lots of unpleasant side effects. There were pros and cons to keeping the status quo, and pros and cons to risking the new drug.

But if the side effects associated with the status quo were awful enough, a person would risk whatever the new drug brought along with it, no questions asked.

I turned on my radio as I often did before slipping into bed, but this time, instead of an oldies station, I thought I'd try something current. I fiddled with the dials a moment until I heard a DJ announce Adele. People at work talked about her, I remembered. I left the dial on that station and turned out the lamp.

Adele sang about a fire starting in her heart.

I thought of the Three Nephites again and realized I finally understood their wish.

I fingered the hard, scaly patch near my nose and thought of all those years without a companion, hiding desperately from everyone I knew. Leprosy no longer seemed like the worst thing in the world. In fact, maybe it was the best.

Miracle at Salt Lake City International Airport

Elder Rogers clung to his Book of Mormon firmly as he slowly inched down the aisle of the crowded aircraft. His was seat 19C, and it looked like that allowed him the aisle. The passengers ahead of him were struggling to stow their oversized bags in the bins above the seats, but Elder Rogers had checked his two bags, packed with his extra suit, six ties, ten white shirts, his garments, and his brand-new journal. He was only carrying his Book of Mormon because he thought it would give him a good opportunity for missionary work on the flight to Salt Lake. Once there, he'd go on to the Missionary Training Center in Provo. He sure hoped his seatmate wouldn't be another Mormon. As a new missionary, ordained only the night before, he wanted to start off on the right foot.

"Excuse me," said Elder Rogers, squeezing past a heavyset woman having difficulty moving into her seat. The flight was full, with probably a hundred and fifty or more people boarding the plane. Elder Rogers wondered how many were Mormons returning home to Utah, and how many more were tourists about to be exposed for the first time to the Salt Lake Temple, at least from the outside.

He seemed to be the only missionary boarding the plane in Kansas City.

On the left side of the plane were seats A, B, and C. On the right side of the aisle were seats D and E. On row 19, seat A was filled by a bald man with a bushy moustache wearing a plaid shirt. Seat B was filled by a young woman in her mid-twenties, dark-haired, wearing a sun dress.

Clearly not Mormon.

Elder Rogers sat next to the woman and buckled his seat belt. This was only his second flight ever. Once, when he was fourteen, he'd gone with his family to Miami to visit his aunt. They'd done nothing but sit in her house and talk the entire three days. Elder Rogers still didn't know any more about Miami than he'd seen in the movies.

Thank goodness for movies.

He thought about *The Other Side of Heaven* and wondered what adventures awaited him in Mexico City. Then, perversely, he thought about *The Singing Nun* and snickered. The woman next to him glanced in his direction.

Elder Rogers pulled himself together.

After another fifteen minutes or so, everyone was seated, and the flight attendants explained all the security features. Most people were reading or looking at their phones, but Elder Rogers had only gone through the drill once before on that previous flight and thought he should pay attention. Not that Heavenly Father would let a plane with a new missionary crash, but it didn't hurt to know these things.

Soon, the plane was speeding down the runway, and despite being far from the windows, he could see enough to grow alarmed at the velocity. So fast, and yet, was it fast enough to get off the ground? The plane was so full it had to be heavy. So many of the passengers were obese. Even he could afford to lose ten pounds. Elder Rogers grasped the armrest tightly and closed his eyes.

"It'll be okay," the woman next to him whispered. She patted his hand.

Elder Rogers turned to look, and suddenly, they were off the ground. His stomach lurched, and he clenched his teeth. But thirty seconds passed, then a minute, and everything seemed fine. The woman laughed.

"I've been on a plane before," Elder Rogers protested.

"You look like a seasoned traveler," the woman responded with a smile.

"Well, maybe not that, not yet. But I'm off to see the world. I'm heading to Mexico for two years."

The woman held up her hand like a stop sign. "I know what you're doing. I see the white shirt and the short hair and that Book of Mormon in your lap, and I don't want to be preached to, if that's okay."

Elder Rogers's heart sank, but he knew it was just a routine obstacle the Adversary was putting in his path. Obstacles were there to be overcome. No good missionary story was without them. "What's your name?" he asked.

The woman hesitated but finally replied. "Roan."

Elder Rogers held out his hand. "I'm Elder Rogers."

Roan shook his hand gingerly.

"So you live in Salt Lake?" he asked.

"I'm heading to San Francisco. Salt Lake is just a thirty-minute layover."

She wouldn't even see Temple Square, Elder Rogers realized. He was her only hope. He was just about to say something else when she held up her hand again.

"I'm sorry. I don't mean to be rude, but I don't want to talk for two hours. I brought a book to read." She held up *Inferno* by Dan Brown. "It's about overpopulation and biological warfare."

The Last Days.

"Can't wait till they turn this into a movie," Roan continued. Then she opened her book and began reading.

Yes, thought Elder Rogers sadly. Hollywood would turn a book called *Inferno* into a movie. Trash was almost the only thing on the screen these days. They didn't make films like *The Sound of Music* anymore. He liked to watch LDS movies, but there weren't very many of them, and some lacked experienced actors. It was almost as if the Lord were testing the faithful.

Elder Rogers turned to look across the aisle, but the gap was too great to hold a conversation with 19D, and anyway, the flight attendants were headed their way with beverages. Elder Rogers opened his Book of Mormon and began reading about the Anti-Nephi-Lehies. He drank a diet 7-Up, walked to the bathroom at the rear of the plane to pee, and squeezed past a large man on his way back to his seat. He read some more, and prayed for Heavenly Father to give him a chance to reach Roan's heart.

She finished her apple juice and went back to her reading.

And finally, they were making their descent into Salt Lake. Elder Rogers shrugged. Getting Roan to agree to have some sisters visit would have made a nice story to tell his first companion. But there would be plenty of missionary opportunities in Mexico. Elder Rogers closed his eyes, tired of reading. Forty minutes later, Roan put her hand on his arm.

"Something's wrong," she said.

Elder Rogers was instantly alert. "What do you mean?" He looked about. Everything seemed normal.

"We keep circling."

"I'm sure it's nothing," said Elder Rogers. The Lord had called him on a mission, after all.

"It's not normal. Something's up."

Elder Rogers wondered how he could use this information to ask Roan the Golden Questions. He was still trying to think of something when the pilot spoke over the loudspeaker. "Folks, this is your captain. There seems to be a little problem with our landing gear. We're not sure we can lock it. Everything is going to be fine, but we're going to be a little late getting into Salt Lake. We appreciate your patience."

Elder Rogers looked at Roan. She didn't look scared, but she was frowning. Elder Rogers found that his own heart was beating a little rapidly.

"I wonder how they'll test the gear," she said, in a matter-of-fact voice. It was probably just his own lack of faith that was scaring him. He needed to show Heavenly Father his trust.

"They'll figure out something," he told her. "I saw this movie called *Freetown*. It was about six Mormon missionaries in Africa. I think it was Liberia. Anyway, there was a civil war, and people were being killed right and left, but God led those missionaries to safety."

Roan looked at him aghast. "So God is going to make sure *you're* okay, and I'm toast?"

Now it was Elder Rogers's turn to look stupefied. "That's not what I'm saying at all! I'm just saying Heavenly Father is going to protect us."

"Because you're here."

"That's not what I'm saying!"

Elder Rogers tried to find a way to lead the conversation back to something constructive, but Roan turned to look past the man sitting on her left and out the window. Even Elder Rogers could see glimpses of the ground far below. Way far below. He prayed, and he felt a spirit of comfort. Everything was going to be okay. He wondered if he should prophesize a safe landing to Roan, and let her be impressed despite herself when it turned out to be true. He might not get her address to give to the missionaries, but he could plant a seed. Sometimes, these things were team efforts and took the work of several people over several years to finally get someone into the baptismal font. He wasn't against sharing the credit.

Fifteen more minutes passed. Roan was talking to the man with the moustache by the window, ignoring Elder Rogers. Elder Rogers looked about the cabin and saw that everyone was perfectly calm. There was nothing to be frightened of. He couldn't wait to tell everyone at the MTC about his adventure.

Then the plane shuddered.

"What was that?" asked Roan. She was talking to him again. "That wasn't landing gear."

A flight attendant walked by quickly, looking worried.

A few minutes later, the captain came over the loudspeaker again. "Folks, everything is going to be fine. I need to let you know we've lost an engine, and we're running low on fuel, so we're going to have to try to land, even if we aren't sure about the landing gear. There's a ninety percent chance that the landing gear is functioning properly and we just aren't able to verify it. But the flight attendants will instruct you on how to prepare for an emergency landing."

"Oh, my god," said Roan.

Elder Rogers thought it best not to reprimand her for taking the Lord's name in vain. Instead, he tried again to turn this into a missionary opportunity. "The Lord will protect us," he said, as calmly as he could manage, with his own heart racing. He thought of another movie he'd seen, *The Cokeville Miracle*, about an incident sometime in the '80's. A disturbed couple had made a bomb and taken an elementary school hostage in a Mormon town in Wyoming. They'd herded over a hundred and fifty people into one room and threatened to kill everyone if they weren't given a ransom of two million dollars per hostage. Before everything was over, both kidnappers were dead, and though a few dozen hostages were injured by the exploding bomb, several of the children insisted they saw angels guiding them to the far side of the room to protect them.

After his disastrous experience mentioning the last movie, Elder Rogers wasn't sure if he should recount this one to Roan. She'd probably make some snide remark about Sandy Hook or something. Perhaps her heart was already too hardened by sin to feel the Spirit. Some people only saw the negative in everything, blind to God's love. But Elder Rogers had been called to get through to exactly those people. He looked about the cabin again. Passengers were on their cell phones talking worriedly to their families. A few women were sniffling. But no one was really panicked.

Families, thought Elder Rogers. Half the people on this plane must be Mormons, he realized. Maybe that was the way to get to Roan. And to the other non-member passengers as well. He might end up converting a whole planeload! He could stand and address the other Mormons. He could lead them in singing some inspirational hymns. Prove to the others that Mormons had faith in God's protection. Or maybe he could get the men to lay their hands on the side of the plane while they all gave the plane a priesthood blessing. He had his vial of olive oil on his keychain.

Elder Rogers could only imagine how everyone would feel after they landed safely after such a blessing. There would be several baptisms for sure. Someone might even make a movie about it. *Miracle at 37,000 Feet.* He hoped they'd get someone good-looking to portray him.

Elder Rogers turned to look at Roan. She was on her phone, crying softly as she said good-bye to someone.

The flight attendants had already told everyone what to do, but Elder Rogers hadn't been paying attention. He could see out the window they were getting a lot lower. But they were still going very, very fast. His chest hurt.

There was another shudder, and the plane dipped dramatically, prompting several people to shout in fear.

Heavenly Father would protect them. Elder Rogers had been called to be a missionary.

The ground was approaching rapidly. And they were going so, so fast. Suddenly, Elder Rogers unbuckled his seat belt and ran to the back of the plane, slamming the lavatory door behind him. He was going to have terrible diarrhea, and he didn't want to embarrass the Church by soiling himself upon landing.

The plane fell, and Elder Rogers felt his stomach lurch as if he were on an elevator descending too rapidly. He heard screams from the cabin and prayed. Then they hit the ground.

When Elder Rogers woke up in the hospital the next day and learned he was the sole survivor, he looked up at the nurses in astonishment and thought about the movie *Unbreakable.* He shook his head in wonder, feeling a searing pain from the movement. He might not be a superhero, he realized, but he was still obviously special. He'd tell his story to everyone in Mexico and convert hundreds. Perhaps thousands.

"God sure loves Mormons," he said softly to the nurse injecting something into his IV line. She raised an eyebrow and glanced at the nurse standing next to her. Elder Rogers turned painfully and felt about for a TV remote on the stand beside his bed. They must have the BYU channel here, he thought, showing things that would be acceptable for a missionary to see. Then he realized with a start that *his* story would be airing in Utah one of these days. He smiled, ignoring the stab of pain emanating from his split lip.

Maybe he'd play himself in the movie after he finished his mission.

Elder Rogers looked at the nurse holding the syringe and noticed she wasn't wearing garments under her scrubs. He smiled again. Then he took a deep breath and asked her the first of the Golden Questions.

Hitting the Send Button

"Good afternoon," I said. "We're missionaries with The Church of Jesus Christ of Latter-day Saints."

The forty-year-old Filipino man I'd stopped on the sidewalk leaned forward slightly to read my nametag. "Missionaries?" he said with a frown. "Do you guys do any good?"

"Well," I said slowly, "we preach the gospel of Jesus Christ, and—"

"But do you do any *good*?" the man repeated.

"We teach people how to live worthy lives," my companion, Elder Matson, interjected. "We help them spend eternity with their families."

"Oh, my god," said the man, laughing. "I sure don't want to be with *my* family for eternity!"

"If you had the Gospel..." Elder Matson began.

"No, thanks." The man held up his hand. "Not interested." He turned and walked away.

Elder Matson looked at me and frowned. "You blew it again, Elder Thatcher. You're never going to make senior companion." He shook his head and we continued walking along Rainier Avenue in south Seattle, looking for someone else to approach. A woman with a white cane walked by quickly on her way to the nearby Lighthouse for the Blind. I watched her navigate down the sidewalk, envying her confidence.

Elder Matson's words had stung. I'd been on my mission for thirteen months and should have been made senior a good while back. I'd had difficulty memorizing my discussions, though, never a bright student. It didn't help that we rarely had the chance to practice the lessons in real life with investigators. The fact that I had yet to baptize a single convert had inspired the mission president to leave me a junior. Even in Seattle, most missionaries had baptized *someone*. I obviously still had important things to learn.

"Please, Heavenly Father," I prayed silently, "help us to find a Golden Contact. Please let something good happen *today*. I ask this in the name of Jesus Christ. Amen."

There were a good many people bustling about, but probably half of them didn't speak English. Many of them were African women wearing head coverings, their drapery so long it dragged on the ground, afraid of showing even an inch of flesh. While I certainly appreciated their sense of modesty, there was clearly no way they were going to be interested in the Church. Others were Latinas I might have tried my faltering Spanish on, but we were forbidden to speak to women without chaperones present. That left the men.

And the men in this neighborhood, if not African Muslims, were African-American men who gave us looks which did nothing to encourage me to approach them. I talked to a couple of Latino men and a few white men, but they weren't any more interested.

"Elder Thatcher, you're dragging me down. You've got to do better."

I'd heard this from most of my companions and wondered sometimes if I should just go home. I didn't want to *hurt* the work, after all. "Heavenly Father," I prayed silently as we continued walking, "please help me." I glanced up into the cloudless sky and went over the points I'd reviewed a hundred times before. "If I go home, it will be a terrible blow to my parents. I'll lose any chance of marrying a respectable girl in the temple. I know I'm wasting my time here. I know I'm wasting your time. I'm throwing away my parents' money. I'm a failure to myself and to the Church and to you. But going home will be an even bigger failure, one I might not be able to recover from." I watched an African man walk into a tiny convenience store. "Couldn't you let me get hit by a car and die on my mission? It's my only hope." A woman wearing a head covering came out of the store. We kept walking. I didn't know much about science or medicine, but I knew enough to realize I was seriously depressed and probably needed to see a shrink. But going to one would be yet one more failure. I needed to be strong. "Please help me, Heavenly Father."

I was just about to close when Elder Matson nudged me and pointed to an Asian teenager. I forced a smile and started to approach. The boy shook his head and turned away.

"Sheesh, Elder Thatcher, can't you even get two words out?"

I tried to return to my prayer, wondering if Heavenly Father kept it on hold when I was distracted, like an email draft. If I didn't manage to end with the words, "in the name of Jesus Christ, amen," I felt as if the prayer didn't leave my mind and reach Heavenly Father. I could be on my knees for twenty minutes during Quiet Hour in the morning, pouring my heart out, but God wasn't really listening until I gave it the seal of approval at the end. The prayer didn't count unless I did it in Jesus' name.

"It's too hard, Elder Matson," I replied. "I can't do this. I'm miserable."

"Oh, for Pete's sake," he returned, disgusted. "Stop whining and buck up. You don't have it so hard. Think of missionaries sleeping on dirt floors in Brazil. Or having to memorize the discussions in Chinese."

I bit my lip and kept walking. My companion was right, of course, but somehow, his words weren't very comforting. My father used to say the same thing if I complained about my summer job mowing lawns in the blistering heat of Birmingham, Alabama. "Think of the people in India who don't even have lawns," he would say. "Think of the people in the Philippines who live on $5 a month. You should be thanking Heavenly Father for your blessings, not moaning about how hard you have it." Then he'd go on a rant about modern teenagers.

My father was probably right, too. I was spoiled. I was ungrateful, not worthy to be a missionary. "Heavenly Father," I began praying. "Please—"

Elder Matson stopped an elderly white man slowly pushing a red wire cart full of groceries. "Good afternoon, sir," he said. "Have you ever thought about where we go when we die?"

"We don't go anywhere," the man replied. He kept walking.

"Don't you want to be with your friends and family again who've gone on before you?" Elder Matson persisted.

"Playing the lottery's a fool's game," was all the man said in return. The odd response made Elder Matson stop and turn to me.

"Be glad you're not him," he said. "At least we have God on our side."

"Couldn't we go tracting for a little while?" I asked. "Stopping people on the street is so hard." At least when we knocked on doors, we had a chance at teaching.

"Complain, complain, complain," said Elder Matson. "You heard President Winter last week. If you had faith, we could be baptizing fifty people a month."

I nodded, and we kept walking. "Heavenly Father," I began again silently, "help me have a better attitude." I watched a teenage girl in green head coverings run to catch a bus. "Help me to have faith. Help me to *help* someone." I saw an Asian man and woman in their sixties heading our way. "Please help me to find the right words. I ask this in the name—"

"Talk to them, Elder Thatcher!"

Darn it. Didn't get to hit Send again.

"Good afternoon," I said, smiling. "We have a message about how to keep families strong in today's world." The woman looked at me blankly while the man shook his head briefly.

"Go on, Elder."

But I let the couple move on. "We're just making people miserable," I said. "Like us."

Elder Matson's mouth fell open. "I can't believe you said that. The gospel makes us *happy.*"

"I'm not happy," I said.

Elder Matson put his hands on his hips. "Elder Thatcher, you need to repent. You wouldn't be so depressed all the time if you just remembered how much better off you are than 99% of the world. You have the Church."

My companion was right again, I told myself. I had to stop being so negative. No one liked Negative Nellies. Not my companions. Not God. Not me. I sent up a quick prayer in the name of Jesus Christ. We kept walking along the street, working up the courage over and over again to stop total strangers. It was late June, and the sun was sweltering. At least ninety degrees. It didn't make me homesick.

I stopped a Latino man who pretended he knew less English than I suspect he really did, and Elder Matson stopped a white man. While my companion often criticized my approaches, his were no more effective, as far as I could see. Of course, Elder Matson gave me the occasional evil eye after being rejected, as if it were somehow my fault, even if he were the one talking. And perhaps it was. Although people passed us every few minutes, our approaches were fifteen or twenty minutes apart. The day was just dragging on.

"Elder, I'm tired," I said. "We've been walking for hours."

"The pioneers had to cross the plains," he replied. "Some of them didn't even have shoes."

"If only we were actually accomplishing something," I said.

"It took the saints forty years to build the Salt Lake temple."

I was going to have to ask President Winter for permission to see a doctor. I'd call the mission home this evening. This couldn't go on.

"Your problem is that all you want to do is reap. Planting and sowing take time. Lehi's family was in the desert for months and months before they set sail for America. Good things don't come easy."

"But Elder Matson," I said, "in thirteen months, I've only taught fifteen lessons."

My companion stopped and put his hand on my shoulder. "Elder Thatcher, my father dedicated two years of his life to the Lord in Norway. And he didn't baptize a single person."

So what good did he do, I wondered?

"Your problem is that you don't realize how good you have it. You could be in Ethiopia right now." He nodded toward a woman walking by wearing a black head covering, her body completely covered in black. In this heat

Religion made people do the strangest things.

I started to speak but waited for a huge Safeway delivery truck to roar past us before it was quiet enough to be heard. Elder Matson was trying to be a good senior companion, but he wasn't helping me. I was sure it was just my depression talking. Or was it my sinful nature? But knowing I was better off than someone else didn't keep me from being unhappy, even if that was just one more moral failing on my part. "When you burned your hand on the oven last week," I pointed out, "you said, 'Dagnabbit!' and started jumping around the kitchen. I didn't see you calmly walk over to the sink to put your hand under the faucet and say, 'I really have nothing to complain about. Some people are burned much worse in car accidents and house fires.' You were saying 'flip' and 'pick' faster than an investigator shuts his door in our faces."

"That's not the same thing."

"I'm unhappy, Elder. I'm not making a difference. I came out here to make a difference."

My companion stared at me a long moment. "I think you need an emergency interview with President Winter."

I nodded. "Can we go back to the apartment?" I asked. "I'm tired."

Elder Matson looked at me for a moment, looked at his watch, and then sighed. "Well, we certainly aren't going to get any work done with *that* attitude." He pointed ahead, and we walked half a block to the nearest bus stop.

An old Asian woman carrying a cloth bag full of groceries was waiting there, as well as two teenage black girls wearing head coverings. Another black woman in her early twenties was also waiting, her hair a twist of bright blue dreadlocks, and her ample shape overflowing her tight clothes. She was smoking a cigarette. "Please, Heavenly Father," I began silently, though I wasn't sure what I was praying for.

Then my attention was caught by an old black man with a walker coming toward us from the opposite side of the street. We weren't at a corner or at a crosswalk. The street was busy, and he was inching his way out in traffic, oblivious to the danger. "Please help that poor man," I prayed.

The black woman with the blue dreadlocks dropped her cigarette and rubbed it into the pavement with her foot, and then she walked out into the street. Holding onto the black man's arm, she held up her other arm to block traffic. Cars stopped, their drivers impatient, for the interminable time it took for them to finish crossing the street. The man didn't thank the woman, and the woman didn't say anything to the man. The old man hobbled slowly off up the street, and the young woman pulled out another cigarette. Elder Matson was looking down the street to see if a bus was coming. I stared at the woman.

She had just done more genuine service in five minutes than I had done in thirteen months. She didn't look any happier than I did, but she didn't look any less happy, either.

"Thank you, Heavenly Father," I prayed.

Would he hear it if I didn't hit the Send button?

Perhaps the way to send a message was to actually *do* something.

The bus was nowhere in sight, but now I saw that something else was. There was a beer bottle on the grass just off the sidewalk. And an empty Cheetos bag. And a plastic cup and a straw. And still more trash.

I leaned over and picked up the beer bottle and deposited it in a small trash receptacle next to the bus shelter. It certainly wasn't much of a contribution to the world, I thought, but maybe I could look for other more substantial opportunities and fit them into my schedule. I couldn't tell my kids fifteen or twenty years from now that the most useful thing I'd done my entire mission was pick up trash on the street.

Or maybe I could.

I reached down to pick up some more.

Donating to a Good Cause

"I'm horny," said Elder Wright, sitting at his desk and tapping his Book of Mormon.

"Well, that's too bad," I replied, sitting at my own desk with my missionary discussions in front of me. I was reviewing them so I wouldn't forget them, on the off chance I might actually teach one someday. "You know we can't masturbate for two years."

Elder Wright laughed. "Two years? We can't *ever* masturbate, Elder Blocker." He stared down at his polished black shoes. "At least before my mission, I could go on dates. A hug and a kiss was better than nothing."

I didn't want to admit that I'd never been on a date. Mormon teens weren't allowed until they were sixteen in any event, and frankly, I'd been more interested in reading books by Michael Crichton. There were some clunkers among the lot, for sure, but some of his stuff would be read a hundred years from now. Spending time with *The Andromeda Strain* was better than dating a girl I didn't particularly like, just to have some human contact.

To be honest, for the most part, I was rather satisfied with having a missionary companion twenty-four hours a day. It didn't keep me from having wet dreams, but at least wet dreams were involuntary. Nothing I had to confess to the mission president. I'd been out on my mission in Sacramento for eleven months now. It had been fourteen months since I'd last masturbated. I hoped to be able to hold out the entire two years. Talk like this wasn't helping.

"What do you plan to do about it?" I asked. "The president asks some pretty probing questions in our interviews. And you blush at the drop of a hat."

"Did you have to use the word 'probing'?" Elder Wright moaned. "I keep thinking of something warm and wet."

"And what would you know about that?"

"We have television where I come from."

"Oh." We had blocked channels back at my home. "Well, you'd better do some sit-ups or something. Lunch period is almost over and we have to get back to work soon."

We spent the afternoon at the park, pestering people with questions they didn't want to hear, much less answer. I'd only baptized one person so far, though Elder Wright had baptized two, impressive since he'd been out three months fewer than I had been. We were both believers, something I hadn't thought would be an issue in the mission field. But I'd already run across two or three missionaries who planned on leaving the Church just as soon as they finished their college education. Too many of them were dependent on their parents for tuition and didn't want to end up mired in student debt. So they were out here paying their dues. It seemed an awful way to live, but I certainly understood flying under the radar.

We did a little tracting late in the afternoon. The only person who let us in was a middle-aged woman, a JW who wanted to argue. We politely excused ourselves and left. We weren't supposed to be alone with women anyway.

Another person, a young woman with a tight-fitting blouse, stood in her doorway and said, "Why don't you plant trees somewhere? Or paint over graffiti? Why don't you teach English to immigrants?" She pointed a finger in our faces. "Get a real job and donate your money to good causes." Then she reached forward and grabbed Elder Wright's crotch. He squealed in terror and blushed. "At the very least, you could donate some sperm to a fertility clinic. You can do that much to help the world, can't you?"

I pulled my companion loose from the girl's grasp and we hurried away. We walked down to the end of the block and stopped at the corner. Elder Wright was sweating. "You okay?" I asked.

"I liked it," he said softly.

"Well, we can hardly start tracting out fertility clinics on the off chance you'll get groped once in a while."

"I want to go back to the apartment and wank off," he said. He looked at me searchingly. "Am I a pervert? Do any other guys ever want to beat off like I do?"

I pointed down the next block and we began walking to the first door. "My bishop back home once told me that every boy who's ever come in his office has done it. All the single adult men, too. He said it was no big deal."

"Yeah?"

"But he was released from his calling two weeks after he told me that."

"Oh."

We knocked at the door. A woman about thirty answered. She wasn't interested. We moved off toward the next house.

"What about girls?" asked Elder Wright. "Do they ever do it?"

I shrugged. "I don't know. I didn't ask."

"Maybe we should bring it up at the next district meeting when the sisters are there."

I turned to look at him and saw he was grinning. "You flipper," I said.

"Makes you wonder, though, doesn't it?"

"What?"

"If men are really more degenerate than women. My Dad says that's why we get the priesthood and women don't. We need it more."

I rang the doorbell. "Doesn't seem to be working very well, does it?"

"No, I heard the bell."

"I meant the priesthood."

"Oh."

We continued tracting for another hour or so without results. Most missionaries hated going door to door, but I actually enjoyed it. It must be somewhat like sitting in a coffee shop with friends. You ate your scone and sipped your coffee to have something to do, but it was all just to grease the wheels of conversation. I had some of my best talks with Elder Wright while we were tracting. He was rather a good guy, when he wasn't talking about his penis.

And sometimes even when he was. These were conversations I could never have with my father, that was for sure. I wished there were something I could do to help him. But we were each all alone when battling our inner feelings.

After dinner, we went to visit some of the active members of the ward, trying to get them to give us names of their friends we could go teach. That wasn't much more successful than stopping strangers in the park, but at least we got a glass of chocolate milk out of it. Finally, around 9:00, we headed for home.

"I'm exhausted," I said, flopping down on our tattered sofa. A member from the Elders Quorum had donated it to the missionaries several years before.

Elder Wright went to the kitchen and spread some strawberry jam on a piece of bread. He stood over me and took a large bite. "I'm tired, too," he mumbled.

We had over an hour before we were supposed to go to bed. We needed to catch up on some Companion Study. Perhaps we'd read an article from the *Ensign*. We had several years' worth of the magazines in each missionary apartment. I'd already gone through half of them. Perhaps there was something on tithing, I thought. Or prayer.

Elder Wright finished his jam and bread and gulped down some water from the faucet. We couldn't afford the milk he preferred.

"Boy, what I really need is a good wank, and then I could sleep all night."

"Oh, for Pete's sake," I said. "Can you give it a rest?" He was going to make *me* horny in a minute.

"It's not my fault," he protested. "Hormones affect your neurons. I read that somewhere."

"In a porno magazine?" I asked.

"No need to sneer. Blue balls is a real condition."

"Go take a cold shower."

Elder Wright frowned and stood staring at me for a long moment. Then he nodded and headed for the bathroom. Five minutes later, I knocked on the door. "Let's keep it snappy in there."

"You'll make a great zone leader someday, Elder Blocker."

I stuck my tongue out at the door.

In the morning, we sat together at the kitchen table eating our Cheerios. Elder Wright cut a banana into slices and dropped them into our bowls. "I had a dream last night," he said hesitantly.

"I expect everyone has dreams every night," I replied, taking up a spoonful of cereal.

"No, I mean, like a dream from God."

I stopped with my spoon halfway to my mouth.

Elder Wright smiled when he saw I was taking him seriously. "It was an answer to our prayers."

"How to find converts?" I asked, putting my spoon back in my bowl.

"No, no," he said. Then he looked about as if making sure no one could overhear us. "How to masturbate without sinning." He smiled triumphantly. But he was still blushing.

I stared at him. "What in the world are you talking about?" I asked. "It's always a sin. Even after you're married."

"But what *if?*" he continued. "What if there was a way?"

"Oh, good grief." I wanted to stand up and walk away from the table. I looked at my companion's hands, his fingers splayed out in anticipation. "All right, what did God tell you?"

Elder Wright leaned forward conspiratorially. "It's what that girl said yesterday. We go to a fertility clinic and donate. It's for a good cause. We're helping people. It can't be a sin if we're helping people." He sat back. "So that's what we do. We donate."

I couldn't believe what I was hearing. Missionaries going to a fertility clinic to beat off? It was absurd.

And yet there was somehow an odd logic to it.

"Let's go today," he said, his face scrunched up. "I'm dying."

"Let me pray about it."

We finished our breakfast in silence, though Elder Wright kept looking at me expectantly every few seconds, making me nervous. After washing the dishes, I kneeled beside my bed and tried to figure out what Heavenly Father thought of my companion's plan. It *couldn't* be a good idea. Could it?

At 9:15, we both got dressed and ready to start our work day. As we stood together to pray, Elder Wright put his hand on my arm. "Well?" he demanded.

"We'll have to go to the library to find where there's a clinic around here," I said.

Elder Wright started jumping up and down. "You're the best companion I've ever had!"

So we did go to the library, and after that, we headed to a clinic on the far side of town, hoping no other missionaries would catch us leaving our area. We took off our nametags and went up to the front desk. A heavy young woman with no make-up looked up at us. Elder Wright nudged me in the ribs.

"We're here…" I said. "Uh, we're here to…"

"Yes?"

"We'd like to donate sperm," Elder Wright cut in.

"Were you referred here by someone?" asked the young woman, as if she heard this every day.

"Not really," I answered.

"How did you hear about us?"

"We went to the library."

"Well, let's hear it for genes that carry intelligence."

Elder Wright blushed.

"It's fifteen dollars," she went on, handing us both a clipboard. I looked at Elder Wright and then started digging in my wallet. The woman put up a hand and laughed. "No, we pay *you*," she said.

After filling out a surprisingly detailed questionnaire and submitting to a blood test, which I admit I hadn't been expecting, we were each led to a separate small room, shown how to deposit our samples, and directed to some well-used magazines sporting women with large breasts and widespread legs. I had never looked at porn before and wasn't about to start now. I thought about the person of my dreams instead and was soon done.

Elder Wright was brilliant, I thought. We'd have to come here every week.

We went back to the park to pester some more people about the Church. Elder Wright seemed to be in a much better mood, and it was somehow contagious. We wrote down the names of two different people who wanted us to stop by their place later to teach them.

We tracted throughout the afternoon, taught a partial lesson, and placed a Book of Mormon. Then we headed back to the apartment for dinner. We had bologna sandwiches with cheese and mustard. "I have to hand it to you," I said. "You were truly inspired."

"Thanks." He chewed a big bite of his sandwich.

"You may end up in the Twelve one day," I continued.

"You're the best companion I ever had," he repeated. He sighed.

Tonight, we visited a couple of inactive families and tried to leave them with some happy gospel thoughts. A teenage boy about fifteen from the second family agreed to come to church on Sunday, if we could get him a ride. "We'll stop to pick you up at 8:30," I said.

"Well, if it's you guys," said his sister, who was a year older than the boy, "I'll come, too."

Elder Wright and I looked at each other, knowing we'd be breaking the rules, but sometimes, you just had to adapt to the situation. I nodded, the kids smiled, and then we left for home.

Back at the apartment, we celebrated our day by having some butter cookies with the last of our milk. "Elder Blocker," said my companion, taking a bite of his cookie, "I feel alive in a way I never have before."

I sipped my milk, not too much, wanting it to last. It was just an orgasm, I thought. Both of us had experienced them before. And yet... "I have to admit, I do, too," I said.

"But you know, it didn't really solve the problem, did it?" Elder Wright's face suddenly fell. "I still feel horny."

Some people were just never going to be satisfied, I thought. I shook my head, but I still knew Elder Wright was a great guy.

"I want to make another donation," he said, staring at the table.

"Right now?" I laughed. "I'm quite sure the clinic is closed."

Elder Wright looked me directly in the eyes. "Will *you* take my donation?" he asked softly, blushing.

I could feel my own face burning now as I stared back at him. A hundred thoughts and feelings collided in my mind. All the different directions my future could take flashed before my eyes. All the different directions *our* future could take.

I stood up and offered my hand. Elder Wright rose hesitantly and took it. "I'm glad you see me as a worthy cause," I said with a weak smile.

Elder Wright's smile flashed brightly in return. "I want to donate regularly." We walked slowly to the bedroom together, leaving the lights on.

And my companion didn't blush once, despite all the surprising new things we did.

Prayer Circle Jerk

I had mixed feelings about being transferred to the mission office in Calgary. On the one hand, I wasn't crazy about proselytizing so it was a relief to do paperwork instead, but on the other, I knew the real reason I was being called to serve as mission secretary was because I'd confessed to President Durham in my last interview that I was gay. I was being kept nearby so he could monitor me closely. I felt the way I imagined a Muslim must feel every time he goes through security at an airport.

The mission home was a mansion, with a master bedroom for President Durham and his wife, a smaller bedroom for the two Assistants to the President, and one for my new companion, already there as treasurer, and myself. In addition, there were offices for the president, for the APs, and for my companion and me. Plus a large living room and a large dining room. And probably a few other rooms I didn't know about yet. I'd been given a tour my first day in the mission field ages ago. The place was a palace.

I arrived around 4:00 in the afternoon after traveling most of the day. I put down my suitcases and rang the doorbell. A moment later, a smiling young man opened the door. It was Elder Benson. He was to be my companion. "Elder Lukins!" he said cheerfully. "Welcome to the mission home! We're all excited to have you here!" He reached down to grab the larger of my two suitcases and motioned for me to follow him. I picked up my other suitcase and walked into the house. There was a grandfather clock in the foyer, near a marble-topped stand upon which sat a crystal vase filled with purple flowers. I followed Elder Benson up the stairs, down the hall, and into our room. He set the suitcase he was carrying beside one of the single beds. I set mine down beside it.

The room wasn't as sparsely decorated as were most of the previous places where I'd stayed. The two Book of Mormon posters of Arnold Friberg paintings actually had frames. And our desks didn't look like they'd been pulled out of someone's trash. There was even a polished mahogany dresser along the wall. Elder Benson saw the look on my face. "Not bad, huh?"

Was tithing money paying for this?

"You'll have to wait to unpack," said my companion. "We need to go out and get a few last things for dinner. Sister Durham wants cherry tomatoes for the salad. She does the cooking, but the elders do all the other housework. She loves it, and it's more fun for us than stopping strangers on the street."

Following Elder Benson back down the hall, we passed Elders Cook and Baldwin, the two Assistants. I'd met them before, of course, but was surprised to see them now without ties. Even Elder Benson's wasn't knotted very tightly. President Durham and his wife were waiting at the bottom of the stairs, both dressed as if on their way to church. The president had served for decades as a pilot in the Air Force before retiring. He and Sister Durham had four adult children, the youngest of which was now serving a mission in Kenya. "Welcome to the mission home," said the president warmly. Sister Durham looked like she wanted to give me a hug, but knowing the rules about contact with the opposite sex, she shook my hand instead.

"I like the little yellow tomatoes," she said as Elder Benson and I headed out the door. "And we probably need another gallon of milk."

My companion and I climbed into the mission van and took off. "Will we be meeting with any members later?" I asked. "Surely, we do *some* missionary work around here." I still needed to do something significant during my time to save my soul. Serving the Lord was only one reason I was a missionary. Another was to make myself stop being so sinful. A selfish reason, of course, but that was the whole point. I was a bad person and needed to be better.

Elder Benson turned toward me and smiled. "Relax, Elder. There is more than one way to serve. The Church would fall apart if we all did only one thing."

I supposed he was right, but buying groceries didn't seem like the kind of service I'd been called out here for. "Heavenly Father," I prayed silently, "please help me to accept your will." Perhaps things were lax because it was Transfer Day. Tomorrow we'd get down to real business. I would be in charge of reading the weekly emails from all the other missionaries in the mission and passing on relevant information to the president. I'd sort through all the stats everyone sent in, see where we needed to improve, which districts needed more stalwart missionaries, which areas we might think of closing. During conferences, I'd take minutes of all the talks and proceedings. I felt guilty even at the thought of no longer proselytizing, but since I'd been so bad at it these past thirteen months, I had to look at this assignment as a blessing. Yes, I'd been put back into junior companion status again, but other than that, maybe I could stop feeling like a failure every day of my life.

That would be easier, naturally, if I wasn't in fact a complete failure.

We bought the yellow cherry tomatoes and the milk and headed back to the mission home.

Dinner was lovely, everyone sitting around a real dining room table with a tablecloth, not the tattererd card tables I was used to. People were chatting happily. No one was bickering as sometimes happened in other missionary households. There was no mad scramble to clean one's plate and get seconds before everything was gone. There was other furniture in the room, an elegant sideboard, vases filled with pink flowers, a framed oil painting. Everything so beautiful and peaceful. Almost like being in the temple. And yet... something was amiss. I couldn't quite put my finger on it until Sister Durham came out with the dessert, a six-layered almond cake with coconut icing. Then it came to me.

There was no guilt in the house.

I was always weighed down heavily with the stuff, but I didn't want to be a jerk and ruin everyone else's happiness, so I smiled and joked along with the others. Maybe this assignment wasn't so much to keep me under watch as it was to offer me a chance to breathe.

"Elder Lukins," said Sister Durham, setting a slice of cake in front of me, "I'm so glad you've come to the mission home. I can tell you're going to fit right in."

Elders Cook and Baldwin nudged each other in the ribs, and Elder Benson clapped me on the back. My companion and I cleared the table, and then the APs washed the dishes. Sister Durham sat on the sofa and picked up her knitting. The president gave her a kiss and headed to his office.

"This is all so strange," I said once my companion and I were back in our room. "It's like having a family again." Only my own family had never been so serene.

"You'll find we're all very close here," said Elder Benson. "You'll be in the mission home for the rest of your mission."

Something about the way he said it made me shiver. People already claimed Mormons were a cult, and I had to admit, the idea had certainly crossed my mind the first time I went through the temple and saw all the odd things there. I casually walked over to the window now and pushed aside the curtain. No bars on the windows, I noted with relief. I wasn't trapped.

And we did have the curtains, didn't we, not just blinds like everywhere else I'd been. I was simply feeling guilty for all the luxury. But it wasn't as if the Prophet and apostles lived in shacks. It was okay to have it easy, I reminded myself. Stop feeling so much guilt all the time.

I pulled out my discussions and started reviewing them. "You won't need to do that anymore," said Elder Benson from across the room. I bit my lip but then put them away and opened my Book of Mormon. Elder Benson looked as if he was about to say something else but instead turned back to his own desk. He was reading a book, too. I strained to see the cover.

Who was Alice Munro, I thought?

I rubbed my arms even though I wasn't cold. Something clearly wasn't right. I had the same feeling I'd had when I'd watched the movie *The Stepford Wives*. People joked that Mormons were like that, perfect yet fake. Looking over at Elder Benson, I wondered just what I'd gotten myself into.

But then I pinched myself for my stupidity. Why did I think going without a tie was a sin? Why did I think reading a book was a sin? There was nothing wrong with any of these people, I realized. I just needed to look at the world with more understanding.

The apostle who'd spoken once at the Missionary Training Center had explained it. "The Lord will guide you every step of your mission. Every city you're assigned to, every companion you live with, all is for your benefit. The Lord takes care of his own." I turned back to my scriptures, while I heard Elder Benson murmur at something he'd just read.

Kneeling beside my bed later, I offered my last prayer of the day heavenward. "Please, Heavenly Father, help me stop being so uptight. All I've done all day is judge everyone, and they've been nothing but nice to me. Help me to relax and finally enjoy my mission. I want to enjoy my life." I remembered the quote: Man is that he might have joy.

It was the whole point of the gospel. The reason for everything.

I climbed into bed and pulled up the covers. I hadn't baptized a single person my first year as a missionary. And now I'd never even have the chance to baptize anyone at all. A cushy life in the mission home wasn't going to make up for returning home a failure. How could I ever feel joy? I closed my eyes and tried to get to sleep.

The next morning, I was surprised to find eggs and sausages on the table. I was used to cereal every morning. Elder Benson and I washed the dishes after all the men were finished. Sister Durham smiled at us from the sofa. I could faintly hear the click of her knitting needles.

"Come on, Elder Lukins, it's almost time for Devotional. It's the most important meeting of the day."

We dried our hands and headed to the president's office. Everyone else was already seated, the padded chairs forming a loose circle in the large room. President Durham wore a tie, but none of the elders did. I actually felt embarrassed now that I was wearing one. Elder Benson and I sat in the remaining two chairs, and then the president stood up. "We'll start with a hymn," he said. "Ye Elders of Israel." We all knew that one by heart and sang the first two verses with a vigorous rhythm.

"And now, we'll go over our plans for the day."

How odd, I thought. No opening prayer. I listened as the APs described a couple of articles they were working on for the mission magazine. Elder Benson explained he'd be going over the lease for one of the missionary apartments that had turned out to be problematic and coordinate with the local district leader to see about finding a new place. Maybe they'd arrange to have the elders rent a room from a member. I blubbered that I'd start sorting through the latest teaching statistics. And then President Durham spoke.

"Got a call from one of the sister missionaries last night," he said. "An empty pot fell off the stove onto the floor. She was afraid there was an evil spirit in the apartment. Took me fifteen minutes to calm her down. Elder Cook, see if you can address this in your next conference talk. The last thing we need is hysterical, superstitious sisters."

I frowned. My first companion had told me about casting out an evil spirit.

The president spoke for a couple more minutes, and then he stood up. He motioned for the rest of us to stand as well. Everyone looked at me and began grinning. Elder Benson turned to me and said, "We begin every day with a prayer circle."

Like in the temple, I thought? Surely, we wouldn't use the sacred handshakes.

We stood up and formed a tight circle, so close that our elbows were touching. We all bowed our heads, and the president offered a prayer. It seemed rather ordinary. I suppose I was expecting the man to be more inspired. Then he said "amen" and I looked up.

What the—?

The other elders had their pants unzipped, their erect penises pointing starkly into the air. I looked toward the president in horror. His penis was in his hands. "Elder Lukins," he said softly. "I know how hard it is for gay missionaries. For gay members of the Church in general. I have a testimony that the Lord has called me specifically to make it easier for us."

The other elders were smiling and gently stroking their penises. Despite the terror rushing through me, I could still feel my groin tighten. "But President…" I said.

"It's okay, Elder Lukins," he replied soothingly. "I've hand-picked the mission office staff. To get not only the gay elders, but the friendly gay elders, the ones we actually want to be around." He smiled. "Things will be different here. You can beat off. You can suck each other." He looked at Elder Benson and winked. "You can do whatever you want. I remember what it's like to be young."

Elder Benson reached behind me and patted me on the butt. Blood was pounding in my ears.

"I myself have serious needs, too," he went on, reaching over to grab Elder Baldwin's penis. "I used to have to rely just on asking personal questions during interviews to be able to get off later, but now…" He wiped a drop of pre-cum from the tip of Elder Baldwin's penis and put his finger to his lips. "Now I can have sex two or three times a day." He chuckled. "You'd think that was a lot. But when you've got a lifetime to make up for, it still isn't enough."

I looked at everyone, still appalled beyond words. They were all sinning terribly. The crime next to murder. They were horribly betraying the Church's trust. God's trust.

Sister Durham's trust.

This was exactly what the Church always said gays were like.

Elder Cook started to groan and soon shot into the air. I watched in dismay as Elder Benson caught the ejaculate and wiped it onto his own penis, using it as lubricant. My own penis was painfully pressing against my pants, sinning of its own accord.

I was a virgin, I thought desperately. A missionary. I was going to marry in the temple. I was going to the Celestial Kingdom. I was here to serve the Lord.

Elder Baldwin pulled away from the president's grasp and reached over to unzip my pants. I should stop him, I told myself. This was evil. This was a heinous sin.

He ran his fingers gently along my shaft.

The president saw the look in my eyes and said sadly, "We're all already damned, you know. What difference does it make?"

Elder Benson groaned and shot into the air in a long arc.

Then it happened. I could feel deep in my heart that what the president was saying was true. The Holy Ghost was bearing witness, powerful even in the midst of all this wickedness. Elder Baldwin squeezed me and wiped the pre-cum from my own penis, offering it to the president, who licked the AP's finger.

"Come on, Elder," President Durham said softly. "The Lord directed me to call you to the office. It's the only way. A few moments of pleasure in this life before we're kicked out of God's presence forever." He held out his hand and nodded. "It's okay. We'll have bodies in Outer Darkness, too." Then he smiled, that same sad smile as before. "I know the Church says that only people in the Celestial Kingdom can have sex, but it isn't so." He looked at the other elders. "What are they going to do to stop us? Threaten to send us to hell?"

I could hardly think with Elder Baldwin's hand on my penis again, pulling gently back and forth. But I'd long suspected this horrific ordeal was all a losing battle. All my prayers and fasting and hard work over the years, and I still wanted nothing more than to be with another man.

I stared at Elder Baldwin's penis, the veins throbbing along the sides. Gays were complete degenerates, just as the prophets said. The Church was clearly true. I should call everyone to repentance. I should report what was happening. Maybe I could still save myself.

But I didn't want to be the jerk in the prayer circle, bringing everyone down. I understood now why there was no guilt in the house. It was because there was resignation instead.

I took a deep breath and sighed.

Then I knelt down in front of the president and opened my mouth. He put his hands on my head and smiled.

Saturday's Worrier

We walked into the donut shop, and I stood at the counter to order three glazed donuts, two for us and one for the inactive member we were about to visit. But then I noticed my companion, Elder Grinnell, looking at two police officers sipping coffee with their pastries. "Please, Elder," I whispered.

He paid no attention to me and approached the two men, both in their forties, both showing signs of having eaten here a little too often. I paid for the donuts and joined my companion. "I see you're enjoying a fresh cup of joe," said Elder Grinnell.

The police officers looked at us and frowned. I wished I could remove my nametag.

"Do you ever feel like slaves to coffee?" Elder Grinnell continued. I wanted to die. One of the officers was African-American.

The two officers looked at each other and then back at us. My companion continued with his "Word of Wisdom" approach, despite the lack of encouragement from the two men. Why had the Lord put me with this guy? Every day was filled with agony as he asked awkward question after awkward question. We'd been together three weeks, and I was praying for a transfer next week. It wasn't often that a missionary was stationed with a companion for only one month, but life in the mission field was tough enough without having to endure this.

Please, Heavenly Father, please, I prayed.

"I'm not interested in your message," the black officer said, taking another sip, "but this is the kind of thing my neighbor Louise likes to hear, so you should probably talk to her."

"Could we get her address?" asked Elder Grinnell with a smile.

To my surprise, the officer gave it to him. Elder Grinnell wrote it down in his notepad, and we went back out to the car.

"Another referral," said my companion, sliding behind the steering wheel. "You'll never make senior until you get your performance up, Elder Parkinson."

"But Elder…"

"You're too ashamed of the gospel," he went on. "You've got to be bold." He pulled out onto the street, forcing another car to slam on its brakes, and we continued on our way.

Be bold, I thought. Elder Grinnell was certainly that. My first week in the district, he'd complained about how much his butt itched. Then, to my horror, he'd pulled his garments down one night, leaned over as he spread his cheeks, and asked me to examine him. "You see anything?"

"It kind of looks like a target," I said, "a large ring right around your…your anus."

We went to the medical clinic in our neighborhood the next day, where Elder Grinnell was diagnosed with ringworm. Rather than be mortified by the whole experience, he took the opportunity to ask the receptionist the Golden Questions. We didn't get a referral, but he did place a Book of Mormon.

I supposed at some point I would get used to all this. A mission shaped us into the people we would be for the rest of our lives. Of course, people told me I'd grow used to the heat here in Pensacola, too, but I'd been in Florida eight months, and it hadn't happened yet.

Soon we arrived at our destination, the home of Deanne Tate, a lapsed member of the Church who Elder Grinnell was determined to reactivate. This was our third visit. At the end of our last one, Deanne had told us not to come back. But Elder Grinnell said he was following the Spirit. He parked along the curb, blocking her driveway.

"Are you sure that's a good idea?" I asked.

"Her car's here," he replied. "That means she's home. Even if she asks us to move so she can leave, it will give us a chance to talk in the driveway. Sometimes, you have to actively create your opportunities. In the old days, missionaries stood on top of soapboxes on street corners and preached."

Thank goodness I'd been born in the latter of the latter days, when life was more civilized.

Or had we simply collectively developed stage fright over the years? Back in the day, missionaries converted people by the dozens and even hundreds. Everything now was measured in single digits. Performance mattered.

We climbed out of the car and headed toward the house.

"You're upset again, aren't you, Elder Parkinson?"

I shrugged.

"Come on. Out with it. You have to at least be bold enough to talk to me, if you can't talk to anyone else."

I turned to him. "Do you always have to push so many buttons?" I asked. All this drama was so...scary. It was exhausting.

"Yes," he said. "Yes, I do. Buttons turn people on. Pushing them gets people awake. If you let folks keep sleeping all their lives, they'll never hear the voice of the Lord."

I frowned. "My other companions didn't do it this way."

"Your other companions didn't baptize as much as I have." Elder Grinnell had in fact baptized a whopping five people in the past year and a half. I had yet to baptize anyone. I'd once scheduled one for an investigator, but he'd chickened out at the last minute.

We stood in front of the door, and I rang the bell. Part of me believed him. I'd been invisible my whole life, always afraid to raise my hand in class in school or at church. I'd never won a scripture chase in Seminary because I was so afraid I had the wrong verse, even when I knew it by heart. I could sing in my bedroom but never even tried out for choir.

I'd even tried recording the Sacrament prayer and then playing it when I had to bless the sacrament, so worried I'd flub the lines in front of everyone.

I rang the bell again.

"You need to learn to live, Elder," my companion persisted. "Be the missionary Heavenly Father wants you to be." He started singing "Humble Way," his favorite song from the play *Saturday's Warrior*. Everyone was excited that a film version was now in production. I'd been too scared to try out for one of the missionary roles when our stake put on the play the year before my mission. I would have only had a handful of lines, but the morning of the audition, I stayed home with cramps.

In my senior yearbook, I was voted Most Likely To Be Passed Over For An Academy Award. Everyone thought it so funny. I'd actually shown up for the first meeting of the Drama Club. But I'd left when everyone had to stand to introduce themselves.

I could have done it.

"She's not home," I said after another few moments.

"Well, let's go tracting for a bit until she comes back," said Elder Grinnell. He walked back to the sidewalk and turned west.

"We're just going to leave the car in front of her driveway?" I asked.

"There's no room anywhere else on the street," Elder Grinnell pointed out.

"How's she going to get back in her driveway when she gets home?"

"Her car's already here, dodo. That means someone picked her up. They'll just drop her off."

Chances were that we'd be finished tracting the street long before Sister Tate returned home, so I shrugged and followed my companion to the first door. Every door approach felt like an audition. And every rejection felt like, well, a rejection. We went up one side of the street and down the other, then crossed back and headed up toward Sister Tate's house again. I was dripping in sweat from the hot sun, and we still had several more houses yet to go.

A plump young woman opened at one door, smiling uncertainly at us. Even an uncertain smile was a good sign, though. It was my turn to say something, and I was just about to open my mouth when Elder Grinnell took over. "You're looking radiant today," he said. "When are you due?"

The woman was of indeterminate gravity, but even I knew never to ask a woman that question. The look on her face told me I was right. "I'm not pregnant," she said coldly.

I wanted to sink right into the ground, but Elder Grinnell wasn't fazed in the slightest. "Would you like to be?" he asked with a smile. "We have a Singles congregation here in town, with all sorts of dances and other activities designed to help young people find the right partner. You could find the man of your dreams."

"Would he be like you?" she asked tartly.

"Could be. Could be," Elder Grinnell replied, still smiling. "But there are dozens and dozens of young men to choose from. It's quite possible you could find someone even better, if that seems possible."

I couldn't believe he was saying all this, but the woman finally smiled back and let us take her name and number. We promised to send the sister missionaries over to tell her more about our message, and invite her to church.

"You do the next two doors," said Elder Grinnell as we walked to the next house.

How did he do it? He could turn any disaster into a triumph. While I seemed to turn every opportunity to interact with the world into another excuse not to succeed. When we reached Sister Tate's house again later, I was going to say something brilliant and get her to come back to church. Or was putting off my brilliance even a few minutes yet another excuse? I should say something clever at the next door. And the door after that. And the one after that as well.

On stage every minute and wanting only to watch, never perform. All the while dreaming of being a performer. I did the approaches at the next two houses. The world continued to be unimpressed by my presence.

When we started down the sidewalk back to Sister Tate's house, I stopped and pointed.

"What is it?" Elder Grinnell asked.

"The car is gone."

We hurried back to the driveway, as if a closer inspection would miraculously reveal the location of the missing car. I saw a curtain move inside the house and knew what had happened. Sister Tate had been home all along and had called someone to tow our car.

Finally, I thought. My companion's charm had met its match. I was almost happy, until I thought of the long walk home in the blazing heat. "What are we going to do?" I asked.

"Catch the bus," he returned. He started off toward the main street, and I hurried to catch up. We found a bus stop a couple of blocks away.

There was no shelter, and it was hot. A Latina woman held her hand over her brow to shield her face from the sun. Two young white teenage boys in backwards baseball caps kept poking each other in the ribs and looking at us. Elder Grinnell walked up to the woman and started up a conversation. Within two minutes, he had her name and address.

Suddenly, I remembered a scene from an old movie about a woman's baseball league. Two of the players were sisters, and one always felt dismissed because her sister outshone her on every occasion. I could still see the look of fear in her face, hear the whine in her voice. Being scared every minute of my life just wasn't getting me anywhere, I realized. I simply had to be more like Elder Grinnell. It was clear that was why the Lord had assigned us as companions.

I approached the two young men and smiled. I couldn't just give a normal approach, though. I always failed at that. I had to say something outrageous like Elder Grinnell did. It was boldness that worked.

It was all an act, but that's what actors did.

"How would you guys like to be missionaries in another year or two when you're our age?" I asked. "You might end up in Korea or Scotland or maybe South Africa or Peru. You get to see the world and also help the world at the same time." I smiled again.

The two young men looked at each other for a moment, and then one of them leaned toward me. This was it, I thought. I was finally becoming a missionary.

The boy pursed his lips and spit in my face. The other boy laughed.

I was on stage at the climax of the play and had forgotten my lines.

But out of the corner of my eye, I saw a businessman with sandy blond hair join the small group waiting for the bus. He must have seen what had just happened. I turned to look at him, and he backed away. Elder Grinnell was still talking to the Latina woman and seemed oblivious to what had transpired. I wiped my face and approached the businessman. He tensed but didn't back any farther away.

"You know," I said, shrugging, "we're really just two bumbling kids trying to do what we think is right. We have an important message about families we'd like to share with your family. Is there a night this week that works best for you?"

The man frowned, looked over at the two boys laughing at us, and then glanced at my companion as well. He peered up the street as if hoping the bus would arrive to save him, but then he finally turned back to me. "You guys have nerves of steel," he said. "I have to give a presentation today, and I'm late because I'm so nervous." He shook his head. "I don't know that I really want to join your church, but I'm willing to let you guys talk to me for a bit." He laughed. "Maybe I'll learn something."

He gave me his card, and fortunately, at that point the bus did arrive, and we all climbed aboard and dispersed to different parts of the vehicle.

I should have felt victorious, I thought, but instead I felt exhausted. All I could see ahead of me was month after month of torture. Wasn't there some other way I could serve God? Something that didn't involve giving sermons to the entire congregation, or teaching in front of a large class. Or acting like an ordained representative who knew what he was talking about. Perhaps we didn't all need to have the same personality.

Did Heavenly Father only like those who could put on a good show?

I remembered flubbing my lines at the veil in the temple.

Elder Grinnell fidgeted on the seat beside me. "All this sweat," he said. "I think my ringworm might have come back. I need you to look at my ass again when we get home."

That I could do, I thought.

As the bus jostled down the road, I wondered what the rest of the day had in store for us. And the following days. And the rest of my mission, no matter who my companion might be. Just what, I wondered, would Elder Grinnell say to the next person we talked to? And the one after that? At best, I realized with a sinking heart, this program was all going to require some significant audience participation.

But there was no Oscar in my future.

I bit my nail and looked out the window. Then I adjusted the tie on my costume and softly began singing a song.

The Chains of Paradise

Karen stirred the mashed potatoes listlessly. Stuart and his family would be here soon. Caitlyn was getting baptized tomorrow. She was eight. The age of accountability. Old enough to decide for herself to become a Mormon.

Karen stared absentmindedly at the clock on the stove. Here she was, sixty-two years old, and only now old enough to make her own decision about the Church. Sixty-two. She watched the clock flip to 5:58.

What had she done with her life?

There was a knock at the door. "I'll get it," Paul shouted from the living room. She and Paul had been married for over thirty-eight years, having met as missionaries in Guatemala. Their temple wedding took place soon after they'd come back to the States. They had five children. Stuart was their middle child.

Karen heard the commotion of greetings in the foyer and started stirring again as the potatoes popped like lava in front of her. All the food was prepared, but she wasn't ready to call everyone to the table yet. She needed more time.

Ha! The thing she'd squandered by the decade.

"Hi, Mom!" Stuart came into the kitchen to give her a hug but stopped a couple of feet short. "You okay?" he asked. "You look sick."

"I'm fine," Karen said with a smile, brushing back a wisp of hair from her forehead.

"Because if you're sick, we'll go home. I don't want Caitlyn to be infected with anything on her big day." The service was scheduled for 7:30 at the ward meetinghouse.

An idea suddenly formed with crystal clarity in Karen's head. She could pretend to be sick! She could get out of going to the baptism!

Then Caitlyn came into the kitchen, all sweetness and beauty, in a cute light blue dress with yellow roses. "I'm fine," Karen repeated, "just a little tired." She reached down and gave her granddaughter a hug. She would lose everything if the rest of the family found out. She stood up and wiped her brow.

"You sure you're okay?" Stuart pulled Caitlyn back to stand beside her.

"Dinner'll be ready in just a few minutes. I made your favorite."

"Meatloaf?" asked Stuart.

Karen smiled. She shooed them out of the kitchen and turned off the oven and burners. She put the steaming corn in one bowl, the green beans in another, and the mashed potatoes in yet one more. The salt, pepper, and butter were already on the dining room table, and now she carried out the three bowls one at a time, setting them down on folded napkins. The meatloaf she set on a red tile. She stood back and looked at the table full of food.

Her highest achievement in life was being a wife and mother. It was a good achievement, of course, but it only counted as an initiation to the real thing, eternal family life. And now that eternal family was never going to happen.

There was no Celestial Kingdom to go to.

"Dinner's ready!" Karen called out, and everyone rushed to the table. Caitlyn sat next to her mother, Barbara, and the two boys, five and six, sat on either side of their father. Everyone had thought Bradley and Franklin might be the last additions to the family, after Barbara suffered two horrendous miscarriages, but she was now five months pregnant with their fourth child and feeling like a real woman again.

Paul offered a prayer over the food, and everyone began serving. The family was smiling and laughing. Life should be good.

But Karen had committed a terribly grave sin the day before. She'd gone online and read the Church essays on race and polygamy. Those were things she never bothered about before because only anti-Mormons talked about them. But now the Church had issued its own statements. And after reading them, it was impossible not to want to know the rest of the story. So she'd Googled.

"This meatloaf is so wonderful," said Stuart. "You're the best Mom in the world."

"Karen, I can just never make it as good as you do," said Barbara.

Karen shook her head. "It's the way *you* cook that your kids are always going to remember."

Barbara looked at Stuart and smiled.

Then Paul cleared his throat, and Karen could sense an impending reprimand, something he'd been doing more and more over the past few years as he grew stricter in his approach to the gospel. What he could have to complain about tonight, she couldn't imagine. "Barbara, do you really think you should let Caitlyn dress like that?" he asked, pointing in Caitlyn's general direction with his fork. "It's bad enough that her name's tarnished now because of Bruce Jenner, but she'll be responsible for her own sins as soon as she gets the gift of the Holy Ghost. You shouldn't let her wear sleeveless dresses."

Barbara looked down at her plate in embarrassment, and Caitlyn stopped eating and stared at her grandfather. Karen felt she was going to pop like the potatoes had on the stove.

"You think she's going to tempt some man at the age of eight?" she asked.

"Caitlyn has to obey the commandments," Paul insisted.

"Do you think she's going to tempt *you*?" Karen said.

There was an immediate hush around the table. Women didn't talk back. And they certainly didn't accuse their husbands of sexual improprieties. No one besides Karen knew the real reason Paul had been excommunicated six years earlier. He'd been rebaptized a year later, and his temple and priesthood blessings had been restored, but it was like trying to remove a glob of black paint from a can of white. It really wasn't possible. Everyone would always see Paul as gray, no matter how annoyingly strict he had grown since. Karen was wrong to emphasize the color of his soul.

She had stood beside him after learning he'd been having sex with other men at truck stops and public restrooms. It had all come out after the arrest. She'd worked for years to build her eternal marriage, and nothing was going to take that away. So she forgave Paul. In a way, the discovery was almost a relief. She finally understood why the sex had been unsatisfactory all these years. She'd figured for the longest time that sex was always bad for everyone, that it was only Satan who made it sound alluring to get people to sin. It was a little disappointing to realize maybe other people were actually enjoying it. But once they were in the Celestial Kingdom, they'd have Celestial sex, and it would finally be wonderful. She knew how to endure to the end.

"We—we thought we'd let her have one last night with the sleeveless dress," Barbara sputtered. "But no more after the baptism."

There was another moment of silence and Karen used the time to think. Strictness was acceptable. It was anyone *not* being strict that was suspect. If she had nearly destroyed a perfect evening with two comments, she knew she could never say what she was really thinking. The family would come apart.

And what could she say, really? Joseph Smith was a con man. The man she'd loved and admired her whole life. He had lied publicly about polygamy time after time. The Book of Abraham had been translated recently by scholars, and it didn't say one word that Joseph Smith said it did. The number of inconsistencies and inaccuracies in the Book of Mormon were so vast that believing the account was true was laughable. Brigham Young spoke as a prophet not as a man when he said all those racist things. And how could the Blood Atonement be a real doctrine? Wasn't that what Christ's atonement was for?

The leaders always said to "doubt your doubts." But these weren't doubts. These were facts.

"We saw the movie *San Andreas* the other day," Stuart said, apparently trying to steer the conversation back to safer topics. "Our neighbor watched the kids."

"It was really good," Barbara put in.

Stuart laughed. "We should watch it at church."

"Why's that?" asked Paul.

"It shows God wiping San Francisco off the face of the Earth for its wickedness."

Paul laughed. Karen wanted to punch him in the nose.

The meal continued with more joking and laughter, and Karen thought it best to keep her mouth shut. She ate small bites, getting up regularly to make sure everyone's water glasses were filled. Bradley and Franklin couldn't be better behaved. And Caitlyn was growing up to be a charming girl. Raising children in the Church was clearly a good thing.

And if Karen told everyone what she was thinking, she would never be able to attend Caitlyn's wedding, or those of the boys, or of any of the other grandchildren. She'd hardly even be part of their lives at all. Everything revolved around church. Jenny was singing in the Primary chorus. Albert was giving a talk. Carson was getting baptized. David was being ordained a deacon. There would be other priesthood ordinations, missionary farewells, and homecomings. And outside of milestones, there was always the constant talk of Relief Society events, preparing Sunday School lessons, and the latest General Conference. There were the regular temple outings. Volunteering at the Bishop's Storehouse, or volunteering to clean the church.

And even beyond that, there was the everyday talk of the Last Days, the approaching Millennium, life in the Celestial Kingdom.

Speaking up would turn her into a coma patient in a hospital room, with family gathered around talking to each other, and she just lying there apart from every conversation.

"Heavenly Father," Karen pleaded silently, "please help me." Then she shook her head in disgust. There was probably no God, either.

"You sure you're okay, Mom?" asked Stuart.

He cared about her *now*, she thought, but she'd be cast off like a worn out shoe if they knew.

"Looks like it's time for dessert," she said with a smile. "Barbara, it's your favorite."

"Lime Jello with strawberries cut up?"

"You got it!"

Barbara clapped.

Karen spent the next few minutes serving everyone, watching them eat happily. She already felt like the coma patient, alert and conscious but unable to speak, everyone thinking she wasn't really there.

She'd wanted to play the clarinet in a symphony, had played all the way through college, until being a wife and mother became her only career option. At least she'd been able to finish college before starting her mission, though, she thought with some satisfaction.

As if it had made any difference.

Maybe if she told everyone what she'd learned, they could all leave together. The idea made her heart start beating faster. Karen looked about at the others eating and chatting happily around the table and frowned. Even if she could do that, she realized, it wouldn't be fair to take from them the one thing they loved most in this world. The saying "ignorance is bliss" was invented for a reason.

She was sixty-two years old, and her whole life had been a lie.

But she wasn't dead yet. She might have another twenty or thirty years left. And she sure didn't want to spend them with Paul. Thank God she didn't have to spend eternity with him.

Maybe there was a silver lining to all this.

"Grandma," said Caitlyn, smiling up at Karen sweetly, "you have your talk ready for my baptism?"

Karen looked into her beautiful face and suddenly couldn't breathe. *Sophie's Choice* wasn't just the story of Jewish suffering.

She wiped at her eyes.

"Mom, are you sure you're feeling okay?"

Karen smiled back at Caitlyn. "Today is the first day of the rest of your life," she said. "So I prepared the best talk ever." Caitlyn grinned happily. "But because this is such a special day, I made you an *extra* treat." Karen stood up from the table and went to the kitchen, pulling out of the freezer a small bowl with one scoop of vanilla ice cream, topped with a hard chocolate covering. She brought it back to the table and set it down in front of Caitlyn. The girl's eyes glowed.

Paul leaned back in his chair and lifted his arms out to the side. "We are so lucky," he said, "to have the Church." He shook his head in wonder, and everyone murmured their agreement. "It brings such happiness to our lives."

Karen thought of the ointment she'd had to put on her herpes lesion earlier, and she thought of Joseph Smith ordering abortions for his polygamous wives.

She leaned over and kissed Paul on the cheek and then sat back down to finish her Jello.

The Danish Danite

I sat there in the mission president's office with my companion, staring in shock at President Helberg. It wasn't simply the history lesson he'd given us on the Danites, a secret band of Mormons who had killed apostates back in Brigham Young's time, facts I'd never heard the slightest rumor about before. It wasn't learning about the target that leaders in Salt Lake had given to President Helberg, a wicked man here in Denver they wanted eliminated. And it wasn't even the fact that Elder Blackwood and I were being asked to commit the execution.

The only thought I could keep clear in my mind was this— God approved of me. He liked me. I was special.

All other concerns paled in comparison.

"With the internet these days," the president said, "it's no longer enough just to excommunicate the heretics to discredit them. They're still around to infect the faithful. The saints must be protected at all costs. The very future of the Church is at stake."

And the Lord was calling *me* to save it, I realized, still stunned. Me, who had confessed so many times to masturbation and sexual thoughts. Me, who was so sure I'd never be good enough for the Celestial Kingdom. Me. Heavenly Father wanted *me*.

"Elder Jeppesen," said President Helberg solemnly, "Elder Blackwood, do you accept the Lord's call to serve?"

My heart was beating fast, and sweat was dripping down my forehead, but I didn't hesitate in my reply. "I'll do whatever Heavenly Father wants me to do."

"And you, Elder Blackwood?"

"Do—do we get the second anointing?" he asked. "Do we get our calling and election made sure? I mean…murder…I need to know I won't be damned to Outer Darkness for eternity."

President Helberg laughed. "You youngsters! I swear. Yes, yes, after you finish the task, one of the apostles will be here to bless you."

"The second anointing in the temple?" Elder Blackwood persisted.

President Helberg looked slightly flustered. "I don't know how you found out about that. We don't teach that officially. But yes, that's exactly what will happen." He turned back to me. "Of course, you both realize you can never tell another living soul about this."

"Sacred," I said, "not secret, right?"

The president smiled. "You understand perfectly." He handed us a typed sheet of paper with Scott Cullen's name and address. He was the man who wrote the blog "Mormon Revelations." "Don't call or email me about this. There can't be any trace to connect us. I will stop by Wednesday night to confirm you've completed the task." It was late Monday morning now. "Elder Boswell from the Quorum of the Twelve is scheduled to arrive on Friday. You'll meet with him at the temple on Saturday."

He stood up and offered his hand. I shook it firmly, as did Elder Blackwood. "I can't tell you how much I appreciate this," I said. It was an incredible blessing. I no longer had to struggle every day for the next sixty years, fighting to stay afloat in a sea of sin. I was guaranteed a spot in the highest degree of heaven. And it wasn't only a blessing for me, of course. I was helping all the members of the Church as well. It was a win-win for everyone.

Scott Cullen was already damned to hell. It hardly mattered when he got there.

"Elders," said President Helberg softly, "don't get caught. You can finish your missions and go on to lead wonderful lives. This is between you, me, and the Lord."

I nodded, and Elder Blackwood and I left the office. We drove back to our apartment in south Denver in silence. Sitting at the kitchen table, we looked at the paper the president had given us. There was a map on the back. Scott Cullen lived in an affluent neighborhood we rarely tracted. Rich people's hearts were so often closed to the Spirit. The man was receiving his Earthly rewards now from Satan, but soon he'd learn how fleeting Satan's promises were.

Wondering how we were going to do it, I felt a twitch in my groin. My first instinct was to feel guilt and try to stop the blood from flowing to my member. But then I had another thought.

I could masturbate every day of my life, and it would no longer matter. That was the whole point of having one's calling and election made sure. I let my penis press hard against my pants.

"Excuse me, Elder." I stood up and walked casually to the bathroom, where I unzipped and felt glorious pleasure that, for the first time in my life, wasn't a sin. Or if it was a sin, it just didn't count anymore, which was the same thing. I shot into my hand and stared at the viscous white liquid. "Thank you, Heavenly Father," I prayed. I could have all the sex I wanted in this life *and* for eternity.

Weak things shall become strong. Or something like that.

When I returned to the kitchen, Elder Blackwood was eating a stale cinnamon bun. He looked at me guiltily for a second but then his expression turned brazen. He'd always had trouble with his weight. I knew exactly what he was thinking. "After we finish," I said, "we'll stop by Burger King and get a shake." I paused, looking into his eyes. "A large." He smiled.

"Let's do it tonight," he said.

"You don't want to plan it out?"

"What's to plan? We go up to his door and stab him with a kitchen knife." He finished chewing his last bite and licked the sugar off his fingers. "I don't want to miss our chance."

At the Celestial Kingdom, I knew he meant.

I nodded, picking up the map. "Well, I know where this area is. It gets dark this time of year around 8:00. We'll show up at 8:30. Be back home by 9:00."

It was barely time for lunch. We scarfed down some peanut butter and jelly sandwiches and then headed out the door. We had to act as if nothing had changed. We drove to a working class neighborhood and began to knock on doors. The responses were the same as always, but after an hour, Elder Blackwood turned to me and smiled. "It doesn't matter anymore, does it?" He giggled. "Even if we never baptize anyone. We did it. We passed the test." He closed his eyes and hugged himself in pleasure. "We aren't failures," he mumbled softly. "We aren't failures, we aren't failures, we aren't failures."

I clapped him on the back, and we headed for the next door. An hour later, we taught a partial first lesson several doors down the street and left a couple of pamphlets.

It was still only about 3:30, but Elder Blackwood stopped me before I could ring the next doorbell. "I'm tired," he said. "Let's go watch a movie."

"What?"

"*Mad Max* is playing. I really want to see it."

Movies were completely against the rules, of course, but I was tired, too, and after all, once we met with Elder Boswell in the Holy of Holies on Saturday, even R-rated movies would no longer be off limits.

What had I done to deserve all this?

Well, nothing yet, I realized. The deed in question was still ahead of me.

It was an enormous extravagance, but we bought buttered popcorn along with our tickets. After the movie, we drove home for dinner, but neither of us was hungry. "We'll just wait for the ice cream shake after we're done," said Elder Blackwood. I nodded. We had some time before we needed to leave, so I opened the scriptures, but then I realized I didn't have to force myself to read that stuff anymore. So, so boring. Still, there was nothing else to do, so I read a few pages from the latest issue of the *Ensign*. There was a picture in it of a woman who looked like one of my Mom's friends. I took the magazine into the bathroom with me.

When I came out, Elder Blackwood was napping on the sofa.

I stood there looking at the magazine in my hand and my companion sleeping. Something didn't quite seem right, and I couldn't figure out what it was, but after a moment, I decided it didn't matter. Everything by definition was right from now on. I let Elder Blackwood sleep until just before 8:00, and then we slipped knives into our flip charts and climbed in the car.

We drove slowly to Brother Cullen's neighborhood and parked a couple of doors down from his house. We said a brief prayer and then walked up to the door. I rang the bell.

And then my heart started beating faster again. What if someone else opened the door? What if he fought back? What if he survived?

Then I thought of Nephi and Laban, and a sudden calm fell over me. Scott Cullen opened the door, shook his head and smirked at us, and without a word, we plunged our knives into his chest, over and over as he fell to the floor. Then we ran back to the car and sped off.

"Oh, my god," said Elder Blackwood. "Oh, my god."

I was about to reprimand him, but then I realized it was okay to say things like that now.

We had to go home and change first before getting our shakes, because we'd gotten some tiny splatters of blood on our clothes. We bundled everything into a large garbage bag and tied it off. The knives we simply washed and put back in the kitchen drawer. We dressed in the clothes we normally only wore on Preparation Day and stood staring at each other. Elder Blackburn's lip was quivering.

"Nephi did it," I reminded him. "It's okay."

"What if I die before Saturday?" he whispered. "Before we go to the temple?"

I went over and hugged him. "It'll be all right. Heavenly Father *loves* us. It's all going to be fine."

"Do you really—"

There was a knock at the door. Elder Blackburn looked as if he were about to cry. I walked over and opened it.

"President Helberg!" I said in surprise.

"I heard the news." He walked in without another word. He surveyed the room quickly and pointed to the garbage bag. "Clothes?" he said. I nodded. He picked up the bag. "I'll take care of this." He took a deep breath. "Now there's just one more thing." He set the bag beside the door and directed us to sit on the sofa. "Elder Boswell asked me to give you the second anointing now."

"What about the temple?"

"I have all the keys necessary for the blessing."

He put his hands on Elder Blackwood's head first and then mine, offering a short prayer, making our calling and election sure. In our grungy apartment, the smell of day-old banana peels coming from the garbage, the words didn't seem to be real, but President Helberg smiled down on us like a proud father. "You guys did it," he said, shaking his head. "Even *I* don't have my calling and election made sure yet."

"Did anyone see us?" asked Elder Blackwood, his brows furrowed.

The president shook his head again. "There are no reports of any witnesses at all." He beamed.

Elder Blackwood and I looked at each other and smiled grimly. I felt the hairs stand up on the back of my neck. Was that the Spirit?

"However, Elder Boswell has asked me something else. Something straight from the Prophet." He looked uncomfortable, and I wondered if we were going to be called on to kill more apostates. The idea bothered me, though I suppose at this point it hardly mattered.

President Helberg pulled a pill bottle out of the pocket of his suit jacket. "You're to take these tonight," he said. "There's no need for you to suffer another fifty or sixty or seventy years of this Earth life. You're to go straight to the Celestial Kingdom."

"Before Judgment Day?" I asked.

"You want us to commit suicide?" Elder Blackwood asked softly.

"It's not a sin anymore," the president reminded us. "It'll be quick and painless, and you'll go on to your glory right now and not have to wait."

So this was the way it was going to end. I nodded slowly. I understood everything clearly now.

"I'll get us some water," said Elder Blackwood, getting up and heading to the kitchen.

"Why are you sweating?" I asked the president.

"I guess you guys can't afford much air conditioning." He chuckled nervously.

"It's elders," I corrected him.

"Of course, of course."

Elder Blackwood came back with two glasses of water and handed one to me. Then President Helberg handed us each ten pills. I didn't ask what they were. Elder Blackwood threw all ten in his mouth at once and took a long swig of water. Then the president turned to me and nodded.

I put the pills in my mouth and drank.

The president's shoulders relaxed. "Now you guys—elders—get to bed, and I'll take care of the clothes." He patted us on the head. "You've done such a wonderful service for the Church."

I saw President Helberg to the door and closed it behind him. Then I put my hand to my mouth and quietly spit out the pills without letting Elder Blackwood see. I slipped the pills into my pocket.

"Let's get to sleep," I said. I walked over to the sofa, hugged Elder Blackwood, and kissed him on the forehead.

"Will it hurt?" he asked.

"We won't even notice a thing," I said.

We turned out the light and climbed in bed, still dressed in our jeans. I waited until my companion's deep breathing told me he was asleep and then beat off onto my sheet. My fate was sealed at this point anyway, I realized. I zipped up, grabbed the keys to the car, and drove a few blocks over to the Burger King, where I ordered a vanilla shake. "This is for you, Elder Blackwood," I whispered.

After I finished, I went back out to the car and pulled out my cell phone. I was just about to call 9-1-1 to tell the police where they could find me, when I turned and saw President Helberg standing there with a gun.

Swimming in the Sound

"What would you like for dinner, Robert?" Cary opened the fridge and peered inside.

I laughed, and Cary gave me an odd look. I suddenly realized he was serious. "We just ate half an hour ago," I said.

Cary nodded and closed the refrigerator. I tried to smile reassuringly. He went back to sit on the sofa, watching a rerun of *Father Brown*. We both enjoyed mysteries. "That guy looks familiar."

"It's Mr. Weasley," I said.

"Oh, yeah."

We had that conversation every time the show came on. But it wasn't as if Cary was completely oblivious. This kind of thing only happened briefly maybe two or three...or now four...times a day, and in an instant, he was back to normal. I was sixty-three, and Cary was only fifty-nine. He had years yet before he could retire, and life had to be increasingly difficult at work. At some point, he'd probably even be fired. He'd already told me of a couple of mistakes he'd made for which he'd been reprimanded.

"Who do you think did it?" asked Cary, nodding toward the television screen.

"We just saw this episode last week on the other PBS station."

"Oh, that's right. All these shows are just the same. They run together. I can't keep them straight."

That was fair enough.

I sat on the sofa next to Cary and held his hand as we watched the program. We'd been together now over twenty-two years, and we still held hands every day. We took walks in our Seward Park neighborhood on the weekends, strolling down to Lake Washington. Sometimes, we caught the bus downtown and walked along the Sound, having clam chowder at Ivar's on the Seattle waterfront. Tuesday nights were French night, where we watched a French film on Netflix and only spoke French. We'd served in separate missions in France decades ago, and Cary even now still remembered the language better than I did.

Wednesday nights alternated between the creperie on Pike and an independent Starbucks in our own neighborhood.

Thursday nights we used to play Scrabble and chess, but the last several months, we'd switched to Backgammon, which took less concentration.

I squeezed Cary's hand.

When the show ended, Cary stood up and walked to the kitchen. "What would you like for dinner?" he asked, opening the refrigerator.

Why couldn't it go back to just two times a day? Why was it so bad tonight?

People with Alzheimer's often lived fifteen years or more with the disease.

"We already ate," I said. I could hear a note of irritation in my voice. I was irritated with myself for being irritated. And afraid of irritating him with my comments.

Cary came back to the sofa and sat next to me. "It's getting worse, isn't it?" he said. He stared at his lap.

"I'm afraid so."

"I'm only fifty-six," he said. "It's not fair."

I didn't correct him.

He took my hand and looked at me. "When do you think I should do it?"

"I don't want you to kill yourself."

"We've talked about this, Robert."

"It'll be okay. They'll develop some new drugs."

"I can see the way you look at me," said Cary. "I may be developing dementia, but that doesn't make me stupid."

Why did I let his minor lapses frustrate me? I was a terrible husband. Cary needed love and patience, not irritation.

It was because ours was a "counterfeit" marriage, I realized. One of the General Authorities, Elder Perry I think, had said so at the last General Conference in Salt Lake. Cary and I certainly didn't watch, but we heard enough reports from other ex-Mormons and even from faithful family members to get the highlights. Gays and lesbians didn't have real love. Their marriages weren't authentic. Even their "lifestyles" were fake.

I'd always tried to have a live and let live attitude toward Mormons after being excommunicated all those years ago. But stuff like that made me hate them, a church led by tottering old men.

"Sweetheart," I said, "tens of thousands of couples go through this all the time. If their love is strong enough to get them through, ours is, too."

Cary's eyes moved slowly up to meet mine. "I'd rather have you mourn me now than be grateful later when I finally go."

"But you don't need to go *yet*."

Cary shook his head sadly. "I've already had three lapses tonight, haven't I? It's getting worse."

I bit my lip.

"I have to go while I still have my wits about me. If I wait too long, I won't be able to take care of this myself. I have to do this now so you don't get in trouble for taking care of it later."

"I would never kill you."

"You promised."

I looked toward the TV screen. *Death in Paradise* was now starting. I didn't want to say what I was thinking. Cary sensed my hesitation and was the one to squeeze my hand this time. "But what if?" I finally said. "What if?"

Cary looked at me and raised an eyebrow.

"What if I never see you again? What if this life is all there is? What if the Church is true and we're terrible sinners and are kept apart forever? What if…?"

"All that is still going to be the case whether it's now or five years from now."

My vision started to grow cloudy as a few tears welled up. Yet neither of us was the type to cry so I blinked my eyes dry. "But I love you. I don't want you to go. We still have some good times left." We still had that Pompeii exhibit we wanted to experience at the Pacific Science Center. We still wanted to see *Dear White People* at the public library where they were showing free films for the community. We still wanted to walk on the Great Wall of China. We had planned to go when we retired.

"It's not even May yet. And the water stays cold here all year round. Hypothermia isn't a bad way to go." We'd discussed this at length, back before Cary had any symptoms. It had all been hypothetical then. If either of us started developing Alzheimer's, or had some other debilitating disease, we'd walk into the Sound or into Lake Washington at night and let the life be chilled out of us. It would spare the sick person for sure but more importantly it would spare the healthy spouse. I'd watched my father grow impatient with my mother who lost her vision to diabetes, and Cary had watched his mother grow to hate his father as he deteriorated from his Alzheimer's.

"What if it's a sin?" I said.

"Then fuck God for making the rules."

"Well, we don't have to decide it right now," I said. "We have plenty of time. How about some ice cream?"

Cary smiled. "Sounds good," he said. "Ice cream for dinner. I'm hungry."

We savored each bite of the French vanilla, and when we were finished, I knelt in front of Cary and unzipped his pants. "Your tongue is cold," he said, laughing. But we warmed it up soon enough. I dragged things out longer than usual, making him moan in anticipation. He kissed me at the end.

As we climbed into bed a few minutes later, I said casually, "Did you forget to brush your teeth?" I knew he preferred brushing in the morning, one of his quirks, but I always thought it was healthier to do it at night as well, and he usually did so even if reluctantly. I'd meant the comment playfully, but Cary looked stricken.

"Did I?" he asked. "Did I forget?"

I wanted to slap myself for being so stupid. "Don't worry about it." I smiled.

Cary pulled the blanket up to his chin. "Will I remember who I am in the morning?" he said, looking at his hands clutching the covers. "Will I remember who you are?" He looked at me, his brows furrowed.

"Of course you will," I said. "No disease progresses that quickly. You're okay. We have a couple of years before we have to worry about anything. Tomorrow night we'll watch the new episode of *Game of Thrones.* And Saturday we'll hike up Mount Si. There are still lots of good things we can do. Relax and go to sleep. Everything is going to be fine. God loves us. He won't let us down." We simply had to savor every day that we still had. What other choice was there?

"But you're thinking 'what if?' aren't you? You're thinking 'when?' aren't you?"

I leaned over and kissed Cary again, and then reached out to turn off the bedside lamp.

"I love you," said Cary.

"I love you, too," I returned. "And the answer is a definitive 'not yet.'"

He nodded uncertainly, and I felt more like a jerk than I'd ever felt before. Why couldn't I comfort the man I loved? It was the absolute least I could do. Real love was strong enough to face anything.

Maybe Elder Perry was right.

We both lay down quietly then, and I listened over the next twenty minutes as Cary's breathing slowly became deeper. What was going to happen to us? Whatever Cary's future in the workplace, my own performance was suffering as I agonized over the situation while at my own job, and this was just the beginning. What would I do when the day eventually came when my husband no longer recognized me? He would no longer remember our trips to Paris. He would no longer remember how we'd met at a French wine-tasting event downtown. He would no longer remember all the French films and novels we'd shared. He'd no longer remember our following recipes out of a French cookbook together.

What if he no longer remembered he loved me?

And the bigger question—what if I no longer remembered I loved him?

I finally fell uncomfortably asleep, welcoming the blackness. I didn't even dream. There was just peace. But at some point probably a few hours later, I felt the bed shake, and my eyes opened weakly. Cary's prostate had been growing larger, and he now got up to pee a couple of times each evening. I was just about to go back to sleep when I heard the front door unlatch, and the squeak of hinges.

I was fully awake now. Was Cary becoming like those old men at nursing homes who wandered outside and got lost? Surely, he wasn't that far gone yet.

The door closed quietly, and I heard the soft sound of Cary climbing down the front steps.

He was going to walk three blocks away to Lake Washington.

I dug my fingers into my blanket until my nails hurt. Not yet, I thought. Not yet. I should get up. I should run after him and tell him I loved him no matter what. I should promise him I'd make life good for him because his being here made it good for me. I should drag him back to bed and make love to him again.

Because I did love him. More than anything else in my whole life.

But maybe what I felt wasn't authentic. I should run out and grab Cary and hold him close for as long as it took to convince him to stay. That's what someone who felt real love would do.

I listened to the silence in the house, stretching across the bed to smell where Cary had been lying.

I was going to be alone forever.

But maybe I'd already been alone all along.

My throat hurt.

"Cary!" I shouted.

I turned over and closed my eyes tightly, burying my face in the pillow, trying to blot out the sound of gently lapping water that seemed to fill my mind to bursting.

About the Author

Johnny Townsend earned an MFA in fiction writing from Louisiana State University. He also has a BA and MA in English, and a BS in Biology. A native of New Orleans, Townsend relocated to Seattle after Hurricane Katrina. After attending a Baptist high school for four years as a teenager, he served as a Mormon missionary in Italy and then held positions in his local New Orleans ward as Second Counselor in the Elders Quorum, Ward Single Adult Representative, Stake Single Adult Chair, Sunday School Teacher, Stake Missionary, and Ward Membership Clerk. In the secular world, Townsend has worked as a book store clerk, a college English instructor, a bank teller, a loan processor, a mail carrier, and a library associate. He has worked selling bus passes, installing insulation, delivering pizza, rehabilitating developmentally disabled adults, surveying gas stations, preparing surgical carts for medical teams, and performing experiments on rat brains in a physiology lab. Townsend has published stories and essays in *Newsday*, *The Washington Post*, *The Los Angeles Times*, *The Army Times*, *The Humanist*, *The Progressive*, *Medical Reform*, *Christopher Street*, *The Massachusetts Review*, *Glimmer Train*, *Sunstone*, *Dialogue: A Journal of Mormon Thought*, in the anthologies *Queer Fish*, *Off the Rocks*, and *In Our Lovely Deseret: Mormon Fictions*. He helped edit *Latter-Gay Saints*, a collection of stories about gay Mormons, and he is the author of 23 books.

Most of those books are collections of Mormon short stories. *The Abominable Gayman*, *Marginal Mormons*, *The Mormon Victorian Society*, and *Dragons of the Book of Mormon* were named to Kirkus Reviews' Best of 2011, 2012,

2013, and 2014. In addition to his Mormon stories, Townsend has written a collection of Jewish stories, *The Golem of Rabbi Loew*, based on his years as a Jew. He has also written one non-fiction book, *Let the Faggots Burn: The UpStairs Lounge Fire*, having interviewed survivors as well as friends and relatives of the 32 people who were killed when an arsonist set fire to a gay bar in the French Quarter of New Orleans on Gay Pride Day in 1973. He is the Associate Producer of the feature-length documentary *Upstairs Inferno*, directed by Robert Camina.

Townsend sang in the New Orleans Gay Men's Chorus for a time and performed in the priests' chorus in the opera *Aida*. He has a collection of Victorian ceramic tiles, wooden dinosaur carvings from Bali, and the entire set of Calvin and Hobbes comic strip compilations in Italian. In addition to speaking English and Italian, he's also studied French, Spanish, Russian, Hebrew, Old English, and American Sign Language. Townsend is an avid movie fan, whose three favorite Hitchcock films are *Shadow of a Doubt*, *Strangers on a Train*, and *Rear Window*. He gives regularly to environmental conservation groups, medical charities, groups that support single-payer healthcare, human rights organizations, and to various documentaries and other projects he finds on crowdfunding sites.

The University of Utah in Salt Lake City has a Special Collection of Townsend material, including all his books, the magazines and newspapers that have published his work, his journals, his correspondence, photographs, and even a portrait painted by a prominent gay artist. ONE Archives in Los Angeles, the national gay and lesbian archive, has his UpStairs Lounge materials and his 20 original gay quilts.

Johnny Townsend is married to Gary Tolman, another former Mormon who served in the same mission in Italy. They still speak Italian to each other regularly.

Books by Johnny Townsend

Mormon Underwear

God's Gargoyles

The Circumcision of God

Sex among the Saints

Zombies for Jesus

Mormon Fairy Tales

Flying over Babel

Dinosaur Perversions

The Gay Mormon Quilter's Club

The Abominable Gayman

Marginal Mormons

Mormon Bullies

The Golem of Rabbi Loew

The Mormon Victorian Society

Dragons of the Book of Mormon

Selling the City of Enoch

A Day at the Temple

Behind the Zion Curtain

Gayrabian Nights

Lying for the Lord

Despots of Deseret

Missionaries Make the Best Companions

Let the Faggots Burn: The UpStairs Lounge Fire

Latter-Gay Saints: An Anthology of Gay Mormon Fiction (co-editor)

Available from BookLocker.com or from your favorite neighborhood or online bookstore.

Follow Johnny on his blog, QueerMormon.com, or on Twitter @QueerMormon

CPSIA information can be obtained at www.ICGtesting.com
Printed in the USA
BVOW02s0028040916

461011BV00001B/79/P